SHADOWS
AND
REFLECTIONS:
JAPANESE LACQUER ART
FROM THE
COLLECTION OF
EDMUND J. LEWIS
AT THE
HONOLULU ACADEMY
OF ARTS

Cover illustration: detail from cat.17.
**WRITING-BOX AND DOCUMENT-BOX**
Signed under the ink-stone *Hokkyō Kōrin* with a seal *Hōshuku*
Eighteenth century

ISBN: 962-7956-04-X

Text by Edmund J. Lewis and Joe Earle
Edited by Joe Earle

Photo Credits
    Honolulu Academy of Arts/Shuzo Uemoto: 5, 77, 81, 82.

    Joseph Ficnor: 1, 3, 6, 7, 8, 9, 10, 11, 13 a-b, 16, 19, 20,
    21, 25, 26 a-b, 27 a-c, 29, 31, 36, 48, 52, 57, 65, 66, 67, 68, 75,
    88.

    Kimbell Museum of Art: 2, 4, 12, 13, 14, 15, 17, 18,
    22, 23, 24, 26, 27, 28, 30, 32, 33, 34, 35, 37, 38, 39, 40, 41,
    42, 43, 44, 45, 46, 47, 49, 50, 51, 53, 54, 55, 56, 58, 59, 60, 61,
    62, 63, 64, 69, 70, 71, 72, 73, 74, 76, 78, 79, 80, 83, 84, 85,
    86, 87.

Printed and bound in Hong Kong

*December 1996*

*Helen.*
*With my grateful thanks for*
*your help.*
*Happy New Year.*
*Ed.*

SHADOWS
AND
REFLECTIONS:
JAPANESE LACQUER ART
FROM THE
COLLECTION OF
EDMUND J. LEWIS
AT THE
HONOLULU ACADEMY
OF ARTS

Honolulu Academy of Arts

"One can rightfully say that [Japanese] lacquer objects are the most perfect to have issued from the hand of man. In the least, they are the most delicate. Their manufacture over many centuries, and even today, remains the glory of Japan."

Louis Gonse, 1886.

# CONTENTS

# FOREWORD

The Honolulu Academy of Arts houses one of the finest Asian collections in the United States. Japanese works were among the first pieces to enter the museum at the time of its founding in 1927 and this segment of our Asian holdings has grown in quantity and quality since that time. The collection is comprehensive in nature, the painting component being especially strong. Of particular note is the internationally acclaimed James A. Michener Collection of Ukiyo-e prints, consisting of over 8,000 impressions.

Over the last seventy years the Academy has presented hundreds of temporary exhibitions which deal with various aspects of Japanese art. These have been drawn from our own permanent collections as well as international sources. Shows have reflected special strengths of the collection as well as areas which are not well represented or are totally absent from our holdings.

Only on rare occasions has the Academy shown a private collection of Japanese art and the museum has never before mounted an exhibition dealing exclusively with Japanese lacquer, a medium not comprehensively represented in the permanent collection at this time.

We are, therefore, especially pleased that Dr Edmund J. Lewis has agreed to share his extraordinary Japanese lacquer collection with the people of Hawaii and our visitors from around the world. The elegant, beautifully crafted works which comprise the collection are excellent examples of the talent and technical virtuosity of Japan's finest lacquer artists. Although a wide range of object types are represented, the collection is especially rich in boxes and cases, many of which relate to the medical profession.

The exhibition encompasses works by a wide cross section of artists whose lives span over four hundred years of Japanese artistic production, including a number of important pieces by Shibata Zeshin. This internationally acclaimed artist is well represented in the Academy's permanent collection and the Lewis examples provide an exciting opportunity for expanding our knowledge and appreciation of his work.

Finally, this publication, which accompanies the exhibition, is both handsome and informative, serving as a permanent documentation of this important collection and its presentation in Hawaii.

Hawaii is known throughout the world as a unique venue for East/West contact. The island of Oahu, where the Academy is located, is in fact called by native Hawaiians the "meeting place", and the ethnic heritage of our people reflects this historic appellation. It is, therefore, a distinct pleasure for the people of Hawaii to "meet" Dr Lewis and his unique collection, a collection which is of special relevance to this island state.

**George R. Ellis**
Director, Honolulu Academy of Arts

# ACKNOWLEDGEMENT

Japanese lacquer objects have been appreciated in the West for over three and one half centuries. In the 17th century, fine lacquer objects were received as very special gifts by high ranking officials of the Dutch East India Company stationed in Japan (see catalog no. 6). Among the prominent examples of these art objects in the Victoria and Albert Museum collection in London is the famous Van Diemen box. The lacquer collection of the 18th century acquisitive, Marie Antoinette, can be seen today in the Musée Guimet in Paris. However, it was in the 19th century, with the opening of Japan and participation of Japanese artists in the great international exhibitions that lacquer art gained widespread interest in the West. Lacquer objects presented to the viewer the highest quality of artistry and craftsmanship coupled with subject matter which taught the history, mythology and religious beliefs of the Japanese people. This combination of aesthetic appeal and insight into a remarkable foreign culture captivated many collectors, and I must count myself among this charmed group. Of course, each collector has his or her own idiosyncratic appreciation of an art form and I must plead guilty to having mine. For me, it is not just simply a matter of craftsmanship. Rather, there is a special beauty to these objects. Japanese lacquer is unique in the way in which light interplays with metallic particles suspended in the lacquer medium to produce a distinctive effect. In a famous essay devoted to the subtle but refined way in which subdued light has played a role in traditional Japanese life, Tanizaki Jun'ichirō (1886-1965) described the appeal of the interplay between soft light and the surface of a lacquer object (Jun'ichirō, Tanizaki. *In Praise of Shadows*. Translated by Thomas J. Harper and Edward G. Seidensticker, New Haven, Conn. Leete's Island Books, 1977). I would not begin to attempt to duplicate the eloquence of this literary sophisticate. Rather, I would direct the viewers' attention to the objects themselves. Perhaps an example that speaks to the issue is the writing box (catalog no. 8) in this collection which has as its subject Mandarin ducks on a river bank. It is night time and the scene takes place in moonlight. Once the observer understands this setting, then the moonlit mist, the shadows and reflections of light on the river, the rocks, the riverbed and the avian subjects can be appreciated. And it can be immediately understood that while intense light might well brilliantly illuminate the metallic grains which make up this picture, this is not what the artist intended. It is the subtle interplay of light and image which commands the best understanding of this scene. Moonlight is a common theme in lacquer art and many objects in this exhibition are best understood when perceived in this appropriate perspective. To me, the ability of Japanese lacquer to utilize a subdued light source is a unique and remarkable property. It is my hope that this exhibition will illustrate this to the viewing public the special beauty of this art form.

This exhibition and this catalog is the product of the labors of many highly competent individuals. It is my pleasure to give my grateful thanks to Joe Earle, formerly Keeper of Far Eastern Art, Victoria and Albert Museum, who wrote the catalog entries, contributed an original essay and edited everything in sight. To him goes my unending gratitude. His broad understanding of Japanese history and art brought a remarkable level of expertise to the project. Julia White, Curator for Asian Art, George Ellis, Director, and the staff of the Honolulu Academy of Arts have fostered and encouraged this project and I thank them for allowing this collection to grace their beautiful institution. To Robyn Buntin, whose idea this was in the first place, my thanks. Robyn's friendship and support have long been a positive force in my life as a collector. Dr Stephen Little, former Curator for Asian Art at the Honolulu Academy and currently Pritzker Curator for Asian Art at The Art Institute of Chicago and Dr Bernd Jesse, Associate Curator of Japanese Art at The Art Institute of Chicago provided friendship, timely professional encouragement and needed expertise, all of which are much appreciated. To Elizabeth Knight and her staff at *Orientations* in Hong Kong goes my unending gratitude. It is always a pleasure to watch gifted and efficient professionals at work and that certainly defines the team in Hong Kong. Lastly, to Helen Follmer and Julia Huston, whose secretarial support kept the project on track, my sincere thanks.

**Edmund J. Lewis**

# WHAT IS LACQUER?

**Edmund J. Lewis**

*East Asian lacquer*

East Asian lacquer is a unique substance, different in many ways from Western artistic media, and an understanding of some of its physical and chemical properties helps explain the creative techniques deployed by the Japanese lacquerer. One area of confusion which might be addressed at the outset is the distinction between East Asian lacquer and the substance referred to as resin lacquer, lac, shellac, varnish or even 'Japan'. Articles coated with resin lacquer were probably seen in Europe before the introduction of articles of East Asian lacquer. It is therefore no surprise that these two distinct substances, both of which can be used as decorative and protective surface coatings, are often confused.

Resin lac is the product of secretions made by certain tree-dwelling insects native to India. The resin is collected from the branches of the trees and, after purification, is dissolved in alcohol. The resulting liquid is shellac or varnish. When shellac is applied to a surface, the alcohol evaporates and the shellac dries, giving the object a characteristic golden finish.[1] East Asian lacquer is completely unrelated to resin lac, being a sap tapped from certain species of the *Rhus* tree, specifically, in the case of China, Korea and Japan, *Rhus verniciflua*. The *Rhus* trees and shrubs are members of the cashew family, and other notable North American members of the *Rhus* family are poison oak, poison ivy and poison sumac. The active ingredient of lacquer sap, urushiol, is the substance responsible for the allergic dermatitis caused by contact with the wax on poison ivy leaves. A tiny quantity can cause the reaction and on wet or cloudy days, when the pores of the leaves are open, it can be set off merely by walking among the trees. The commonest traditional antidote was the crushed juice of a little freshwater crab, a cure which has also been known in China since

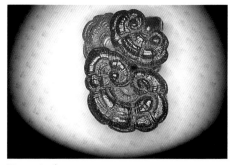

very early times, but most artists appear to become unreactive to lacquer by virtue of the anti-allergic effects of constant exposure to urushiol. In fact, despite the toxic properties of *urushi*, the shoots and nuts of the lacquer tree can be pickled and eaten, and the untreated nuts were used as horse-fodder during the Edo period (1615-1868).[2]

*The Properties of Japanese Lacquer*

Japanese lacquer has unique biochemical and physicochemical properties. When refined lacquer is applied to a surface it does not evaporate and dry. Rather, in proper conditions, lacquer hardens, a phenomenon illustrated by the netsuke illustrated in Figure 1a. Netsuke are toggles which allowed the Japanese to hang various containers from the belt of their pocketless kimonos. They were usually carved from ivory or wood but this particular netsuke, representing a *reishi* [tree fungus], was carved from a solid cube of lacquer. Scrutiny of this object reveals that the original lacquer block from which it was carved was made up of numerous alternating thicker bands of black and brown lacquer (Figure 1b), each of them in turn made up of many thin layers of lacquer. The extreme thinness of each layer of lacquer can be seen at the base of the fungus, where the artist appears to have simply alternated single applications of brown and black (Figure 1c). A

Figure 1a, b, c:
Netsuke [hanging toggle] made of solid lacquer by Kyūsai (1879-1938). The inscription on this object's original storage box reads *Shōwa hinoto-u chūshun* [mid-spring 1927] *Kyūsai kore wo koku* [Kyūsai carved this].
Sealed *Kyūsai*, 2.0 x 2.6 cm

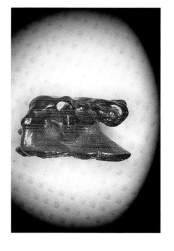

single layer of lacquer has been estimated to be less than 0.05 mm. thick (approximately one five-hundredth of an inch).[3] As this netsuke is 20 mm. tall, at least 400 separate applications of lacquer were required before the artist had a block of lacquer of ap-

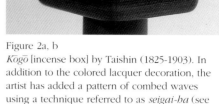

Figure 2a, b
*Kōgō* [incense box] by Taishin (1825-1903). In addition to the colored lacquer decoration, the artist has added a pattern of combed waves using a technique referred to as *seigai-ha* (see catalogue nos. 7, 67). 2.9 x 5.7 x 6.9 cm

propriate size for carving. The rapidity of the hardening process varies according to several factors including ambient humidity and temperature, the presence or absence of a variety of additives used to control the speed, and the quality of the lacquer, but at least one day was probably required for each of these layers.[4] The artist could therefore not even begin his carving until more than a year had passed while the lacquer block slowly grew and developed. A second example of an object carved from a solid block of lacquer is the *kōgō* [incense box] in Figure 2a. The artist, Ikeda Taishin (1825-1903), developed the block of lacquer by alternate applications of thin layers of red, black, orange, yellow and green lacquer. The box was then hollowed out and carved from the solid lacquer block. The lid of this box has a domed shape which causes the plane of the surface to enter various layers of the original lacquer block at different levels, resulting in a multicolored, marbled pattern (Figure 2b).

One may wonder why a lacquer block could not simply be constructed by pouring lacquer into a mold, and it is here that the idiosyncratic properties of lacquer can be reviewed. As noted, the active compound in lacquer is a chemical known as urushiol. Urushiol belongs to a family of organic compounds known as catechols. The basic organization of the carbon atoms which comprise the architecture of this molecule results in a hexagonal structure. As long as the urushiol is present as individual hexagonal units, lacquer remains liquid. Under certain conditions the individual urushiol hexagons interact to form long chains of hexagons, that is, polymers. It is this process of polymerization (i.e., plasticizing) which is the chemical basis for the hardening of lacquer. Since polymerization of urushiol will only take place in the presence of oxygen, atmospheric oxygen must penetrate the surface of the lacquer for hardening to occur. This requires a very thin, uniform layer of lacquer. If the lacquer is too thick, oxygen does not readily permeate the material and it remains liquid. Another important condition is humidity. Apparently the permeation of the surface of lacquer by oxygen is enhanced by a highly humid condition at the surface interface.[5] Around 85 percent relative humidity is ideal, but lacquer will not harden at all when the ambient conditions are dry.

*The Decoration of Japanese Lacquer*

A biological catalyst, the enzyme laccase, is present in the lacquer to enhance the ability of oxygen to promote polymer formation. This enzyme is active only in an acid medium. For this reason, many agents which might be added to lacquer for the purpose of coloring cannot be used because they either alter the requisite acid environment of the lacquer or directly inactivate the enzyme so that it cannot act as a catalyst.[6] The palette of lacquer is thus dependent upon the suspension of chemically inert materials within this medium. In place of conventional coloration, the Japanese lacquerer has therefore resorted to the *maki-e* [sprinkled picture] technique. This uniquely Japanese procedure involves the suspension, incorporation or sprinkling upon the surface of wet lacquer of a range of metallic alloy powders containing gold, silver and copper. The basic varieties of *maki-e* are *hiramaki-e* (flat *maki-e*), *takamaki-e* (high *maki-e*) and *togidashi-e* or *togidashi maki-e* (polished-out *maki-e*). In *hiramaki-e* the design is traced with a fine brush in *urushi*. Before this lacquer has completely dried, the lacquered area is sprinkled with metal powders and after the lacquer is thoroughly set, another layer of lacquer is often applied. When this in turn has set the design is polished. In *takamaki-e* the design is built up in a mixture of lacquer with powdered clay or sawdust before the final *maki-e* decoration is applied. In *togidashi-e*, the completed *hiramaki-e* design is covered with several layers of lacquer, which are polished down to produce a brilliant flat polychrome effect with unusual depth of field. *Nashiji* is another *maki-e* technique often used to cover large areas that are otherwise undecorated, for example the bases of boxes or the insides of lids. The gold used in *nashiji* takes the form of irregular flakes of thin foil, rather than powder, and these are sprinkled into the wet lacquer so that they fall at different angles before they are covered with several further layers, creating a rich aventurine effect.

*Pigmentation*

The pigments which were available to the lacquer artist have traditionally been limited to black and red. Black lacquer resulted from the suspension of either ferric acetate or lamp black (charcoal). Ferric acetate was produced by dissolving elemental iron in vinegar. The black color imparted by ferric acetate, an organic salt, tended to fade and take on a brown color due to decomposition upon exposure to light over many years. This accounts for the brown coloration of many earlier pieces. If the trunk of the lacquer tree is cut too deeply during the tapping process ferric acetate blackening can occur accidentally because of the slight iron content of the trunk. Blackening with charcoal or lamp soot is of poorer quality but can be used to colour the under and middle coats on high-quality pieces.

The color red is derived either from *bengara* [ferrous oxide] or from naturally occurring mercuric sulfide. *Bengara* is the cheaper of the two and in fine lacquerware it is generally used only for the underpainting of *maki-e* designs. Mercuric sulfide is also known as cinnabar or vermilion. Cinnabar, used for artistic and decorative purposes, was officially recognized as an important commodity during the Edo period: the Tokugawa government had among its highest councilors a Superintendent for the Cinnabar Monopoly. His position was equal to senior ministers in charge of precious commodities, such as those who were responsible for gold and silver.[7] Chinese lacquer artists also tended to employ the colors yellow, brown and green, but this was not popular in Japan. Shades of yellow and yellow-brown apparently derived from the use of naturally occurring sulfides of arsenic (orpiment). The sources of the color green were naturally occurring chrome, and copper derivatives.

Several other pigments were occasionally employed. Saratani Tomizō, a contemporary lacquer master, has kindly provided a list of chemicals used for the coloring of lacquer. These include chrome oxide (green), orpiment (arsenic sulfide; yellow), red ocher (hematite or ferric oxide), chrome yellow (lead chromate), Prussian blue (ferric ferrocyanide), bismuth oxychloride (white), and titanium oxide (white). Further information on this subject can be gleaned from the work of J.J. Rein, who wrote one of the early descriptions of Meiji-period Japan. His book *The Industries of Japan* was first published in Leipzig in 1886.[8] Rein had lived in Japan and spent from January to May of 1874 studying the art, technique and chemistry of lacquer. He records that lacquer of green color could be obtained by a mixture of the sulfide of arsenic, orpiment, with indigo. Indigo, probably the oldest known coloring agent, is chemically an indole which is soluble in water and stable in acid media. It is surprising that this vegetable dye would be stable in the unfriendly lacquer environment, but under special conditions of preparation this may have been feasible.

The color blue is rarely found in lacquer objects. Older objects appearing blue may be the result of the suspension of lapis dust in the lacquer. Most lacquer objects which are of the color blue date to the Meiji period (1868-1912), although Prussian blue (ferric ferrocyanide) had entered Japan earlier by way of the Dutch trading colony on the island of Deshima. This chemical dye was used for coloring woodblock prints and probably accounts for blue lacquer objects produced during the early nineteenth century. The other pigments employed have been reviewed by Winter.[9] They include white: (chalk, calcium carbonate); 'lead white' (lead carbonate, lead hydroxide); blue: (azurite); green (malachite and copper chloride). Burmester notes that chalk, lead white, azurite and malachite may decompose in the acidic environment of *urushi* and are therefore not stable.[10] During the process of decomposition not only is the pigment altered, but the *urushi* become less acidic in nature (that is, becomes more alkali). This alteration in acidity diminishes the catalytic activity of the enzyme laccase, which decreases the urushiol polymerization reaction, preventing the lacquer from hardening properly. This accounts for the limitation of palette available to the lacquer artist. It should be pointed out however that in rare instances a lacquer artist may have experimented and determined conditions in which one or other of the above materials could be successfully used as a lacquer pigment. This would account for an occasional rare artistic result.

This brief review has demonstrated that the physical characteristics of lacquer endow it with unique artistic potential, but that its use can also impose severe technical restrictions. These have been overcome by elaborate techniques of application and polishing developed over more than a thousand years, enabling the Japanese lacquerer to turn the textural and visual properties of the medium to his advantage, resulting in the production of enduring works of art.

NOTES

1. Abrams, H.N. (pub.), *Lacquer: An International History and Illustrated Survey* (New York, 1984), 12-14.
2. Matsuda Gonroku, *Urushi no hanashi* [About lacquer] (Tokyo, 1964), 37-49; Abe Ikuji *et. al.*, *Shitusugei nyūmon* [An introduction to lacquer art] (Tokyo, 1972), 42-4.
3. Garner, Harry, *Chinese Lacquer* (London, 1979), 23.
4. Kumanotani, J., 'The Chemistry of Oriental Lacquer', in Bromelle, N. S., and Smith, Perry (eds.), *Urushi* (Proceedings of the Urushi Study Group, June 10-27, 1985, Tokyo; Marina del Rey, Calif., 1988), 243-51.
5. Burmester, Andreas, 'Technical Studies of Japanese Lacquer', in *ibid*, 163-88.
6. Du Yumin, 'The Production and Use of Chinese Raw Urushi and the Present State of Research', in *ibid*, 189-97.
7. Miner, Earl, Odagiri, Hiroko, and Morrell, Robert E., *The Princeton Companion to Classical Japanese Literature* (Princeton, 1985), 476.
8. Rein, Johannes Justus, *Japan nach Reisen und Studien im Auftrag der Königlich Preußischen Regierung*, ii. *Land und Forstwirtschaft, Industrie und Handel* (Leipzig, 1886) [English edn.: *The Industries of Japan* (New York and London, 1889)].
9. Winter, J., 'Pigments in China - a preliminary bibliography of identifications', in ICOM Committee for Conservation, Seventh Triennial Meeting, Copenhagen, II: 84.19. 11-13.
10. Burmester, *ibid*.

# LACQUERERS AND SIGNATURES

**Joe Earle**

Newcomers to Japanese lacquer are often surprised to find that so many examples are signed, and that the signatures can sometimes include a great deal of information when compared with, say, the rather dry and businesslike marks found on Chinese porcelain or English silver. The collectors of the golden age – the Frenchman Louis Gonse, the Englishman Michael Tomkinson, and William and Henry Walters in Baltimore – were as fascinated by the names on their lacquers as they were by the dazzling range of techniques used to decorate them. In these more sceptical times, however, we are apt to question just how much we can reasonably expect to learn – if we want to – from the meticulously executed characters seen on the majority of pieces in every fine collection. By way of introduction to Japanese lacquer of the Edo (1615-1868) and Meiji (1868-1912) periods, this brief essay sets out to introduce some different categories of signature and to explore in greater depth a case-history which throws light on the changing ways in which signatures have been viewed inside and outside Japan.

Over the last century the study of Edo lacquer has often proceeded faster in the West than in Japan. After the pioneering work of the connoisseurs mentioned above, Henri L. Joly's landmark catalogs and other works published in the first two decades of this century gave confidence to two further generations of collectors, while more recent work by American scholars, in particular Andrew J. Pekarik, has increased our understanding of the cultural background to lacquer and its relation to the arts of painting and poetry. On the biographical front, E. A. Wrangham's *Index of Inrō Artists* has gathered together almost everything there is to be known about the lacquerers of the period and their signatures.[1] In Japan, there has recently been a welcome shift of focus away from the classical lacquers of the Kamakura to Momoyama periods (1185-1615) and towards the serious study of such interesting but shadowy figures as Ogawa Haritsu and Hara Yōyūsai, as well as of lacquers associated with the great painters Hon'ami Kōetsu and Ogata Kōrin. The last few months have even seen the appearance of the first genuinely new lacquer-artist index compiled by a Japanese specialist for over sixty years, although as a mark of the different weight given to signatures inside and outside Japan, it is a much shorter work than Wrangham's, and includes far fewer names.[2]

The author of this new index, Takao Yō, usefully distinguishes four categories of artists in a way which may help clarify our future attitude towards their signatures and, perhaps, help us to make up our minds whether they can add significantly to our enjoyment of Japanese lacquer.

1 Artists known from both documentary evidence and from signed pieces.

2 Artists whose names we know from documentary evidence, but whose signatures have yet to be found on pieces.

3 Artists whose names are often found on pieces, but for whose career there is no documentary evidence.

4 Artists whose name is rarely found on pieces and for whose career there is no documentary evidence, although it seems likely that they are distinct artists who actually existed, rather than mere signatures.

A glance at Takao's list suggests that category (3) predominates, closely followed by category (4), with category (1) in third place. Dr Lewis's group of eighty-eight lacquers bears out these statistics, and is also typical of high-quality late-twentieth-century collections in that a small number of well-known artists in category (1), in particular Ogawa Haritsu (21-25 and 27), and Shibata Zeshin (67-82), account for over a third of the pieces. The thirty-five or so names represented include rare unknowns such as Hisamine (catalog number 36), Jisei (20), Shigesato (13), Tōkō (32), or Oyama (2, 62); frequently-encountered unknowns such as Mizutani Shūtōho (30); recorded representatives of great lacquering dynasties such as the Koma (4, 37, 40, 42, 49, 51, 58) or Shiomi Masanari (53-5); and famous individuals including Ogata Kōrin (17-18) as well as Haritsu and Zeshin mentioned earlier. Each of these artists is discussed at the appropriate point in the catalog which follows, but a few general remarks are appropriate here.

Least problematic, perhaps, are the 'rare unknowns'; these signatures make no pretensions to fame and can simply be judged on their merits with the hope that, in time, enough examples can be gathered for a judgement to be made as to whether the signatures do indeed represent a distinct artistic personality – always assuming that this would aid our understanding and appreciation of the pieces they made or decorated. The 'frequently-encountered unknowns' are similar, and it is probable that in the heyday of faking, from the late Meiji period to the early Showa period (c. 1880-1930) there was little incentive for such names to be copied. In the case of the great dynasties, it has long been recognised that in many cases successive generations used the same name for a century or more, and that the fame of the Koma, Kōami, Yamamoto Shunshō and Shiomi Masanari dynasties encouraged the routine use of their names. In any event, the recent researches of Heinz and Else Kress have established that artists from all of the great families, and others besides, could use the same design and execute it in much the same way.[3]

If this interchangeability of designs leads us to feel that a Koma or Kōami signature, whether authentic or not, neither adds to nor takes away from our enjoyment of a box or inrō [medicine-case usually made up of several interlocking sections], stronger emotions are aroused by the names of Ogata Kōrin and Ogawa Haritsu. Because of Kōrin's towering stature as a painter – some would say the greatest exponent of the quintessentially Japanese decorative approach to painting – scholars have argued at length about Kōrin's role in lacquerwork, without ever reaching a firm conclusion. Did he personally apply lacquer at least to the famous 'Kōrin' pieces in Japanese collections? Did he just suggest designs? Or did he have nothing to do with lacquer at all, but simply inspire a lacquer style that was imitated by other artists? The last suggestion seems extreme, and is surely contradicted by the fact that the term 'Kōrin lacquer' covers not only a distinctive style but also a distinctive group of lacquer techniques.

There seems no reasonable doubt that Kōrin's near-contemporary Ogawa Haritsu or Ritsuō (1663-1747) did decorate many of the lacquers signed with his name. The only difficulty, and it is a great difficulty, is to determine which pieces with his signature are his work and which are not. Haritsu started life as a haiku poet in the circle of the great Matsuo Bashō (1644-94) but when he was more than fifty years old he seems to have embarked on a second career as a maker of boxes and inrō decorated with both lacquer and a combination of pottery, shell, ivory (some of it stained), and coral overlays. His design motifs, including imitation ink-cakes, poems, and other Chinese motifs, are often learned and obscure. Much of his work was carried out for the daimyō [feudal lord] of Tsugaru in northern Japan, Nobutoshi (1669-1746) and a few pieces in Japan can be securely tied to this period of the artist's life, the most famous being a set of paper- and writing-box decorated with a deer, an owl and Chinese poems by Nobutoshi himself, carried out in Ritsuō's favourite techniques.[4]

The present catalog includes a large group of pieces with Ritsuō's various signatures or in his style (catalog numbers 21-7). Like all lacquers claiming his authorship they should be treated with caution, but we feel confident that several of them have an excellent chance of being from his hand. It is only rarely, in fact, that we are able even to say that a lacquer in his style is definitely *not* his work, but this seems to be possible in the case of one piece in this book, the inrō (catalog number 24). It is an almost exact copy of one signed *Ritsuō* in the collection of Tokyo National Museum but is instead signed *urushi Setsuzan* [lacquer by Setsuzan]. Setsuzan (also read Sessan) seems to be a name used by another famous lacquerer, Hara Yōyūsai, but there is still room for doubt about the exact identity of the artist, since the association of the two names, Yōyūsai and Setsuzan, is only supported by signed objects and not by any documentary evidence – in other words, this is a category (3) signature for a category (1) artist! Perhaps Setsuzan was a signature used by one of the two further generations of Yōyūsai, as recorded by Takao and assigned to his category (2). There is a further mystery: both inrō are given a fictitious Chinese date, but the date on the Ritsuō is a calendrical impossibility, while that on the Setsuzan is correct. Could this scholarly artist have made such an elementary blunder?[5]

There is less ambiguity about the identity of the two seals *Tenrokudō* and *Kenkoku* on the box (catalog number 26) in Ritsuō style with a roundel depicting Daruma, the founder of Zen Buddhism, but the story of the two artists and the box's subsequent history make a fascinating case-study in the shifting patterns of

Japanese and Western taste in the second half of the nineteenth century. The relationship between Miura Ken'ya (Tenrokudō) and Itō Sadabumi (Kenkoku) was described in an article written in 1916 by Takeuchi Kyūichi, a friend of Kenkoku.[6] Takeuchi starts by tracing Ritsuō's artistic succession, telling us that his leading pupils were Mochizuki Hanzan (mid-eighteenth century, see catalog number 29) and Rissō Kyozan (1736-1802), but there is a problem even with this innocuous-sounding statement. Although Takeuchi would have us believe that Kyozan lived on until 1830, it has been conclusively demonstrated that he was born in 1736, died in 1802 and was not a direct pupil of Ritsuō but of Hanzan.[7] Be that as it may, Takeuchi also marks 1830 as the year in which the direct artistic succession from Ritsuō came to an end. It was also the first year of the Tempō era, when draconian economic reforms imposed by the bureaucrat Mizuno Tadakuni (1794-1851) temporarily made life difficult for the makers of miniature items such as *inrō* and other luxury lacquerwares. By the Kaei era (1848-54) the effect of the Mizuno reforms was no longer so keenly felt, and it is to this time that Takeuchi dates a revival of the Ritsuō style by Kichiroku (or Kitsuroku) and his nephew Miura Ken'ya (1825-89), who combined *raku*-style pottery with lacquer.

An important influence in the Ritsuō revival was the shopkeeper Maruya Rihei, an inspirational businessman who is also said to have prompted Shibata Zeshin's revival of the *seigaiha* technique (see catalog numbers 7 and 67). Maruya was famous for various kinds of bag, purses, wallets for paper handkerchiefs, and tobacco-pouches, of which he sold more than thirty with silver chains to a single client in 1857,[8] suggesting that conspicuous consumption was back in vogue. It was this leader of fashion who took up Miura Ken'ya and reintroduced the Ritsuō style.

> One day [Takeuchi writes] Maruya Rihei happened to see some *raku* ware by Miura Ken'ya. Finding it very interesting he summoned Ken'ya to his house, showed him some examples of *Ritsuō saiku* and got him to recreate the style by using both *raku* pottery and *maki-e*. Maruya Rihei's *Ritsuō saiku* got gradually more fashionable and came to be widely accepted. One of the *tairō* (daimyo elders) of the day, Ii Naosuke (1815-60, Lord of Hikone, who also had connections with Zeshin) wanted to have a new Ritsuō-style bookcase made. To find the best man for the job, he consulted with a tea-master who frequented many daimyo residences, and Ken'ya was commissioned as a result of this man's advice.

> The reason for this choice was that Ken'ya was a man of tea, of independent spirit and acquainted...with many leading lights of the cultural scene. At the time he was living in Chōsen-nagaya, Asakusa, where he made the bookcase. It was very similar to one which Ritsuō had made for the Lord of Tsugaru. I am not sure whether the copy is still in the possession of the Ii family, but the design for it was handed down to my friend Kenkoku Itō Sadabumi. Because Ken'ya was originally a potter, his lacquerwork was rather undeveloped, so he learned the craft from Sadabumi, a resident of Fukagawa. This Sada was a skilled craftsman who often carried out Ken'ya's commissions. As well as learning from him he taught him lacquering, but for some reason things ended badly between them. Sada assumed the name Teiji [actually the name of a different artist who worked in both lacquer and pottery] and, taking advantage of the prevailing fashion, made pieces in the Ritsuō style.

> Ken'ya's version of *Ritsuō saiku* is a combination of Kenzan-style ceramics and miniaturist lacquerwork. He sold most of his works as his own, and never made fakes of Ritsuō. Towards the beginning of the Meiji period my friend Itō Sadabumi became a pupil of Ken'ya and, taking the name Kenkoku, studied Raku pottery and *Ritsuō saiku*, but because Ken'ya was already keen on the work of [the genuine] Teiji he was reluctant to pass on many of his own secrets to Sadabumi.

Apart from the curious repetition at the end of the narrative, this tale seems convincing enough and although parts of the box are apparently of earlier date, the presence of the two seals appears to confirm that its makers had no intention to deceive.

When the British designer and theorist Christopher Dresser visited Japan in 1876-7, Ritsuō's work was sought after by foreign collectors and had assumed an importance, almost as great as the prints of Hokusai or the painting of Kōrin, which was to last for at least a decade. Somehow or other a prevailing sub-current of

Japanese fashion, which under normal circumstances would already have been tailing off, had been taken up by Westerners as part of the mainstream of Japanese design history. Dresser was aware that Ritsuō's work was being faked and he obviously placed some of Zeshin's exercises in his predecessor's style in this category:

Some works of this great manufacturer [he wrote in 1882] have come to this country [Britain]. But the majority of pieces which reach Europe are made by Ikede [*sic*] Zeshin, a man who still lives, and who has not only adopted the style of his predecessor, but makes deceptive imitations of the older work; even the cracks and chips of the old specimens being counterfeited.[9]

Unusually well-informed and sympathetic as he was, Dresser made the error of thinking that Zeshin and his leading pupil Ikeda Taishin (see catalog number 69) were a single person; he was also confused about the nature of the 'antique' as seen in Ritsuō's work, since Ritsuō's own work copying Chinese ink-cakes and sticks often reproduces *their* 'cracks and chips'.

At some point between the manufacture of the Daruma box in about 1875 and an exhibition at the Burlington Fine Arts Club in London in 1894, it had been transformed from a virtuoso recreation of the Ritsuō manner into an early masterpiece by one of his predecessors. It was owned by the great British connoisseur Michael Tomkinson and was included and illustrated in the sumptuous catalog of his collection, published in 1898.[10] The cataloguer, E. Gilbertson, wrote: 'Kenkoku was a pupil of Kenya (Kenzan's brother, Ritsuō's master)', a statement that is at best only two-thirds true. Kenkoku clearly *was* a pupil of Ken'ya and Takeuchi tells that Ken'ya *did* have a brother called Kenzan or Kenzō (written with a different *zan* from the famous potter), but the assertion that these three figures lived in the seventeenth century and that Kenkoku taught Ritsuō is pure invention. Tomkinson owned another box jointly made by Ken'ya I and the lacquerer Shōhōsai Kōzan, dated 1848 and inscribed *after a design by Haritsu*, and a similar unsigned box in the Khalili collection, with a design of the Seven Sages of the Bamboo Grove in pottery against a strongly-grained wood surface, is a further indication of the vogue for pieces of this Ritsuō-esque type.[11]

Michael Tomkinson was not the last Westerner to be led into believing in the existence of non-existent early lacquerers. In 1909 Alexander Moslé ascribed an *inrō* in his collection to 'Kiūkoku, teacher of Ritsuō, about 1700' although no such person is recorded in any Japanese source and the signature is likely to be that of Nomura Kyūkoku, a well-known nineteenth-century lacquerer who worked in a general Kōrin-Ritsuō manner.[12] Although there is nowadays a greater willingness to accept documentary evidence on the rare occasions when it is available and reliable, the fanciful tales and over-optimistic attributions we find in the catalogs of earlier collections should warn us not to be too sure that our own opinions will stand unchallenged for long.

NOTES

1 Major works by the scholars discussed here are listed in the Bibliography, pages 194-6.
2 Takao Yō, 'Kinsei makie-shi meikan [A list of Edo- and Meiji-period *maki-e* artists]', *Rokushō*, 17-20 (1996).
3 Kress, Heinz, 'Inro Motifs, Part I', *Netsuke Kenkyukai Journal*, 14/2 (Summer 1994), 24-37.
4 Kyoto National Museum, *Ritsuō saiku* [Inlaid lacquerwork by Ritsuō] (Kyoto, 1992), cat. no. 1.
5 *Ibid.*, cat. no. 24.
6 Takeuchi Kyūichi, 'Ritsuō seisaku no kōkeisha [The inheritors of the Ritsuō style]', *Shoga kottō zasshi* [Painting and antiques magazine] (Apr. 1916), 25-9.
7 Pekarik, Andrew J., *Japanese Lacquer, 1600-1900: Selections from the Charles A. Greenfield Collection* (exhibition catalog, New York, Metropolitan Museum of Art, September 4-October 19, 1980; New York, 1980), 91 and n. 62.
8 Dilworth, David and Rimer, J. Thomas (eds.), 'Saiki Kōi', in *The Historical Fiction of Mori Ōgai* (Honolulu, 1977), 365.
9 Christopher Dresser, *Japan: Its Architecture, Art and Art Manufactures* (London, 1882), 352.
10 Gilbertson, E., *et al.*, *A Japanese Collection Made by Michael Tomkinson* (London, 1898), cat. no. lacquer 471.
11 Gōke, Tadaomi, Hutt, Julia, and Wrangham, E. A., *Meiji no Takara, Treasures of Imperial Japan, Lacquer* (London, 1995), cat. no. 49.
12 (Anon.), *Ausstellung Japan. Kunstwerke. Waffen. Schwertzieraten. Lacke. Gewebe. Holzschnitte. Sammlung Moslé* (Berlin, 1909), cat. no. 1708.

1

## WRITING-BOX

6.4 x 25.5 x 20.0 cm.
Unsigned
Sixteenth-early seventeenth century

This writing-box depicts the Ōmi hakkei [Eight Views of Lake Biwa], a group of scenes owing its origins to the Chinese painting tradition. The original Chinese landscapes, known as the 'Eight Views of Xiao and Xiang' after the Xiang River and its tributary the Xiao which empty into Lake Dongting in Hunan Province, were a popular subject in Japanese painting of the Muromachi period (1336-1568). They were gradually supplanted, however, by a set of analogous Japanese views around Lake Biwa, Japan's largest lake a few miles east of Kyoto. The themes are retained so that, for example, 'Autumn Moon at Lake Dongting' becomes 'Autumn Moon at Ishiyama'. As with much East Asian landscape painting, depictions of both sets place greater emphasis on poetic evocation than on topographical accuracy. The interior of the lid is decorated with plants of the four seasons including plum, peony, chrysanthemum, 'Chinese bellflower', bamboo and willow. In keeping with the Chinese origin of the landscape decoration, this writing-box is in a somewhat Chinese-inspired shape with a base raised on four legs, a form that was later copied by Ogawa Haritsu (see catalog numbers 21-7).

The full set of 'Eight Views of Lake Biwa' is as follows:

*Ishiyama no shūgetsu* [Autumn moon at Ishiyama]
*Seta no sekishō* [Evening glow at Seta]
*Miidera no banshō* [Evening bell at Miidera Temple]
*Hira no bosetsu* [Evening snow on Mount Hira]
*Karasaki no yau* [Night rain at Karasaki]
*Yabase no kihan* [Boats returning from Yabase]
*Awazu no seiran* [Bright sky and breeze at Awazu]
*Katata no rakugan* [Wild geese alighting at Katata]

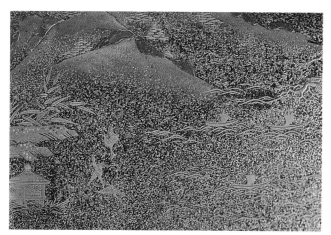

Evening snow on Mount Hira

Bright sky and breeze at Awazu

Evening glow at Seta

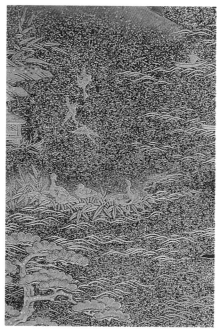

Wild geese alighting at Katata

2

## INCENSE-CEREMONY SET

Storage box: 18.0 x 21.5 x 16.3 cm.
Signed *Naniwa no jūnin Oyama zō* [made by Oyama of Osaka]
Nineteenth or twentieth century

In common with several other cultural pursuits of earlier aristocratic origin, the incense ceremony or game became popular among the townsman class during the Edo period (1615-1868). The competitive aspect of the event increased in importance as participants vied to show off their sophistication and culture by recognizing the subtle characteristics of a variety of rare imported incense-woods. This set is made up of a main storage box and various smaller items including a miniature *jūbako* [tiered box], a footed tray, a box containing boxes to hold the counters (somewhat like playing-cards) for recording the players' guesses, and a set of implements for arranging the incense and ash.

The subject is the *Ōmi hakkei* [Eight Views of Lake Biwa] also seen on the writing-box, catalog number 1. For Oyama, see catalog number 62.

### Reference:

Gōke, Tadaomi, Hutt, Julia, and Wrangham, E. A., *Meiji no Takara, Treasures of Imperial Japan, Lacquer* (London, 1995), cat. no. 116, signed *Oyama*.

Pekarik, Andrew J., *Japanese Lacquer, 1600-1900: Selections from the Charles A. Greenfield Collection* (exhibition catalog, New York, Metropolitan Museum of Art, September 4-October 19, 1980; New York, 1980), 39-40.

3

## WRITING-BOX
3.8 x 20.5 x 23.0 cm.
Unsigned
Seventeenth century

The Ishiyama Temple (see catalog number 4) is shown in Chinese-style perspective, with the foreground at the bottom of the scene and objects further away appearing progressively higher in the composition. On the inside of the cover is an image of an abandoned carriage partially hidden in the mist. This is an allusion to the *Genji monogatari* [Tale of Genji], the famous eleventh-century prose romance by Lady Murasaki Shikibu (see also catalog numbers 4 and 88). Chapter Four of *Genji* is entitled *Yūgao* (literally 'evening face'), the name of a night-blooming white flower, and describes the encounter of Prince Genji with a beautiful woman whom he takes to a deserted mansion to spend the night. The night ends tragically with the lady's sudden and mysterious sickness and death and the Prince's subsequent melancholy which almost leads to his own demise. The unhitched and abandoned carriage is the vehicle which has taken the lovers to their assignation and awaits the happy return which never eventuates.

The combination of this *Genji* theme with a depiction of the Ishiyama Temple refers to a tradition that Murasaki Shikibu (died *c.* 1015) wrote part of her literary masterpiece at that site while viewing Lake Biwa in the moonlight. A little side-room at the temple, known as the *Genji no ma* [Genji room] contained an ink-slab she is said to have used and a Buddhist sutra supposed to be in her own handwriting.

The box is unsigned. An almost identical design of the Ishiyama Temple appears on a box exhibited at the Red Cross Exhibition in 1915 and attributed there to the sixteenth century.

**Reference:**
Chamberlain, Basil H., *A Handbook for Travellers in Japan* (London, 1901), 397-8.
Joly, Henri L. and Tomita, Kumasaku, *Japanese Art and Handicraft, Loan Exhibition Held in Aid of the British Red Cross* (London, 1916), lacquer no. 1 (pl. LXVIII, no. 1).
Pekarik, Andrew J., *Japanese Lacquer, 1600-1900: Selections from the Charles A. Greenfield Collection* (Exhibition catalog, New York, Metropolitan Museum of Art, September 4-October 19, 1980; New York, 1980), 16.

4

## STORAGE CABINET

32.4 x 32.8 x 23.2 cm.
Signed *Koma Kyūhaku*
Early nineteenth century

This cabinet probably depicts the Ishiyama Temple, founded in 749 and located near the southern end of Lake Biwa, just east of Kyoto. In the eleventh century, Murasaki Shikibu is said to have composed the *Genji monogatari* [Tale of Genji] while looking out over Lake Biwa (see also catalog number 3).

There were at least six artists of the Koma dynasty of lacquerers who used the art-name Kyūhaku, the last of whom died in 1816.

**Reference:**
Wrangham, E. A., *The Index of Inrō Artists* (Harehope, Northumberland, 1995), 157-8.

5

## WRITING-BOX

3.9 x 20.4 x 21.7 cm.
Unsigned
Sixteenth-early seventeenth century

This writing-box is decorated with a landscape scene based on the mountains of Sarashina in present-day Nagano prefecture to the north-west of Tokyo. The design continues on the reverse of the lid, where a number of silver characters are incorporated in the design. These give the complete text of an anonymous poem from the *Kokinshū*, an imperially-commissioned anthology compiled in AD 905:

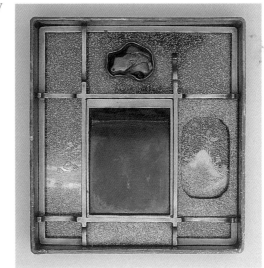

*Waga kokoro*
*nagusamekanetsu*
*Sarashina ya*
*Obasuteyama ni*
*teru tsuki wo mite*

Ah, Sarashina
I cannot calm my troubled heart
As I gaze upon
Mount Abandon-Granny lit
by the bright full moon.

Like many thirty-one syllabled *waka* poems, this one has a double meaning: *Obasuteyama* is a real geographical feature whose name indeed means 'Abandon-Granny Mountain', but *(w)obasute*, taken with *kokoro* [mind, heart] in the first line, could also mean 'leave one's thoughts behind' or 'set aside one's worries'. The full moon is a Buddhist subject, her round shape often likened to complete enlightenment, but according to one traditional interpretation of the poem, people who had abandoned their aged grandmothers to die on this remote mountain would be filled with remorse when they saw the moon shining down, and would return the next morning to rescue their grandparents. In most editions of the *Kokinshū* the syllables *Obasute* are written in phonetic script, leaving the meaning open, but on this box they are written with characters meaning 'old woman' and 'abandon'.

The integration of flowing, half-hidden, calligraphy into a pictorial scheme, called *ashide-e* [reed-hand picture], has been a common practice in both lacquer and painting since the twelfth century, but in early examples whole lines of the quoted text are omitted and must be inferred from the elements of the design. In later periods the poem is often, as here, given in full.

### Reference:

Fukazawa Shichirō, *Narayama bushi-kō* [A study of the warrior-monks of Narayama] (Tokyo, 1956).
Saeki Umetomo (ed.), *Kokinshū* [A Collection of Poems Ancient and Modern] (Tokyo, 1958), 878.

6

## STORAGE CABINET

30.4 x 43.0 x 38.0 cm.
Unsigned
1630-50

This cabinet is an especially fine example of the type of lacquerware manufactured in Japan for the Dutch market from about 1620 until the end of the seventeenth century. A small number of these lacquers, mostly in rather unusual shapes and dating from the 1630s, seem to have been especially commissioned as gifts by officers of the Dutch East India Company and manufactured by members of the Kōami family (see catalog number 43). The landscape panels on the present piece match these special commissions in the exquisite quality of their lacquer decoration and their curious mixture of Chinese, Japanese and other foreign styles.

The subject-matter of the decoration includes many of the favourite motifs of early export lacquerware: improbably tall stone walls topped by pavilions; rocks and waves that have much in common with lacquers for the domestic market; owls; and minutely depicted plants including *nadeshiko* [Dianthus superbus, see catalog number 88] and *tachibana* [mandarin orange]. There is a border of very delicate shell inlay in a key-fret pattern of Chinese or Korean origin, framed by a gold edge decorated with formalized sixteen-petaled chrysanthemums.

**Reference:**
Earle, Joe, 'Genji Meets Yang Guifei: A Group of Japanese Export Lacquers', *Transactions of the Oriental Ceramic Society*, 47 (1982-3), 45-75.

Detail

Detail

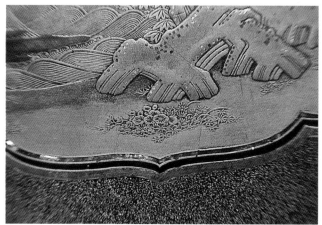

Detail

Detail

7

## WRITING-BOX

3.5 x 22.0 x 19.0 cm.
Unsigned
Late seventeenth-early eighteenth century

The cover of this writing-box depicts Polynesian coral divers on a rocky shore pounded by vigorous waves. Above are dark and forbidding clouds which give the sky a distinctly abstract pattern. The waves and clouds are formed using the combing technique said to have been developed during the Genroku period (1688-1704) by Seigai Kanshichi, who somehow accomplished an illusion of the color blue in the swirling combed pattern. This may account for the technique's Japanese name *seigaiba* [blue-sea waves], although that term has a much earlier literary origin. The technique was lost with the death of Kanshichi and revived by Shibata Zeshin (1807-91) in the 1840s (see catalog number 67).

**Reference:**

Earle, Joe and Gōke, Tadaomi, *Meiji no Takara, Treasures of Imperial Japan, Masterpieces by Shibata Zeshin* (London, 1996), 42.

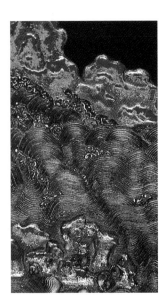

Details of (*seigaiba*)
[combed wave pattern]

8

## WRITING-BOX

4.5 x 21.0 x 23.0 cm.
Unsigned
Seventeenth-eighteenth century

Mandarin ducks symbolize conjugal fidelity, making this writing-box suitable for inclusion in a set of lacquered wedding gifts. This depiction of ducks in the moonlight encourages the observer to view the box in subdued light to appreciate the mist and shadows depicted by the lacquer artist. The interior of the lid continues the river scene with the same regular geometric patterning of the waves, reflecting the pervasive influence of the style of Ogata Kōrin (1658-1716, see also catalog numbers 17-20).

9

## WRITING-BOX

5.7 x 22.0 x 23.5 cm.
Unsigned
Eighteenth century

Wild geese are depicted as a slight mist rises above the shore. On the underside of the lid a gaunt plum-branch blossoms over a bamboo fence, heralding the coming of spring. The gilded *suiteki* [water-dropper] is in the form of a pile of clam-shells.

10

## WRITING-BOX

2.9 x 17.5 x 17.5 cm.
Unsigned
Nineteenth century

A field of autumn grasses seen against a low lying autumn moon
is often portrayed in Japanese lacquer art. The plants shown here
include the chrysanthemum together with six from a set of seven
plants popular since the eighth-century poetry anthology *Man-yōshū*: *susuki* [miscanthus grasses], *fujibakama* [Chinese agrimony],
*hagi* [bush clover], *kuzu* [arrowroot vine], *ominaeshi* [patrinia], and
*kikyō* [Chinese bellflower]. The spiders' webs are inscribed with two
characters reading *kumo* [spider]. The round ink-stone, rimmed in
gold, represents the autumn moon.

**Reference:**

Japan Society and Suntory Museum of Art: *Autumn Grasses and Water:
Motifs in Japanese Art from the Suntory Museum of Art* (exhibition
catalog, New York, Japan House Gallery, fall 1983; New York, 1983), 26.

## 11

**WRITING-BOX**
21.5 x 18.4 x 3.5 cm.
Unsigned
Eighteenth century

The Chinese magician Kinkō (Chinese: Qin Gao) is depicted in raised gold lacquer riding a carp in carved translucent tortoiseshell over gold foil; its eye is of inlaid shell. The waves are depicted in silver lacquer.

Qin Gao is supposed to have lived in the state of Zhao at the end of the Zhou dynasty (traditional dates: 1122-255 BC) or perhaps in the Han dynasty (206 BC-AD 221). Sent into exile by the king of Zhao, he wandered with his many followers to the bank of river, dived in and eventually emerged at an appointed hour riding on the back of a carp. He later dived in a second time and was never seen again. The story is recounted in *Liexian zhuan* [Stories of the immortals], an illustrated edition of which, *Liexian quanzhuan*, was published in China in 1600 and appears to have had a considerable influence on Edo-period (1615-1868) decorative art.

**Reference:**
Eskenazi Limited, *Japanese Netsuke from the Carré Collection* (exhibition catalog, June 15-July 9, 1993; London, 1993), cat. no. 17.
Oriental Ceramic Society, *Chinese Ivories from the Shang to the Qing* (exhibition catalog, British Museum, May 24-August 19, 1984; London, 1984), 49 (pl. 11-14).
Shu Xincheng and others (ed.), *Cihai* [Chinese dictionary] (Shanghai, 1947), 897.

12

## BOX

7.2 x 21.0 x 25.0 cm.
Signed on metal plaques *Yōyūsai* with a *kaō* [monogram] and *made by Hamano Noriyuki*
Early nineteenth century

Kanzan (in Chinese, Hanshan) and Jittoku (Shide) were two legendary monks of Tang dynasty (618-907) China. They lived in the kitchen of a monastery and spoke a private language. Because of this they were considered mentally unbalanced. Kanzan is shown reading a scroll to Jittoku, who holds a broom. The ultimate source of this classic depiction of the two recluses has not been identified but it probably derives, by way of woodblock-printed book-illustrations, from an ink-painting by one of the great masters, Chinese or Japanese, of the thirteenth to fifteenth centuries.

Hara Yōyūsai (1772-1845/6, see also catalog number 24) was a lacquer artist whose work was especially influenced by the Rimpa revival painter Sakai Hōitsu (1761-1828). Noriyuki II (also called Kuzui, 1771-1852) was a celebrated member of the Hamano family of distinguished metal workers, who often collaborated in the manufacture of *inrō*.

The signature is followed by a *kaō*, a kind of individual cursive monogram often called *kakihan* in Western literature.

**Reference:**
Tanaka, Ichimatsu *et. al.* (ed.), *Suiboku bijutsu taikei 4: Ryōkai, Intara* [A collection of ink-painting 4: Liang Kai and Intuoluo] (Tokyo, 1978), nos. 20, 39, 95-6, 108-9.
Wrangham, E. A., *The Index of Inrō Artists* (Harehope, Northumberland, 1995), 153, 340.

13

## DOCUMENT BOX

11.7 x 21.0 x 41.0 cm.
Signed *motome ni ōjite Kashōsai Kakuzan Suga Shigesato saku* [made to order by Kashōsai
Kakuzan Suga Shigesato], with a red seal
Nineteenth century

The cover of this box depicts an *oi* [monk's back-pack], hat, fan and staff with a Siddham
inscription. On the inside of the lid is a *horagai* [conch-shell], used as a signal horn,
and a partially unrolled Buddhist sutra whose minute characters can be clearly
discerned.

Behind the sutra is a sheathed sword, the combination of these two motifs symbolizing
the dual nature of the *yamabushi* [warrior-monks], members of the Shingon and Tendai
sects of esoteric Buddhism. The *yamabushi* would roam the mountains, practising their
religion and taking part in the many civil wars of the medieval period until they were
ruthlessly suppressed by Oda Nobunaga (1534-82), the unifier of Japan. In 1571 he
'ordered his principal retainers to set fire to and to destroy all temples, halls and quarters
on Mount Hiei and to annihilate all monks and inmates' of the Enryakuji, the great
Tendai temple to the north-east of Kyoto.

The Walters Art Gallery owns an elaborate box in the shape of a helmet also signed
*Kashōsai Shigesato*.

**Reference:**

Boyer, Martha, *Catalogue of Japanese Lacquers* [in the Walters Art Gallery] (Baltimore, 1970), cat.
no. 230 (pl. 77).
Tsunoda, Ryusaku *et. al.* (ed.), *Sources of Japanese Tradition*, vol. 1 (New York and London,
1964), 305.
Wrangham, E. A., *The Index of Inrō Artists* (Harehope, Northumberland, 1995), 97 (*s.v.* 'Jiun').

Detail of an inscription on the staff:
The Siddham-script characters
represent a *dharani* [religious
invocation] in the Sanskrit language
which quotes the "Six-Syllable
Manjuśri Spell" invoking freedom from
evil and suffering. It reads: Āḥ vi ra
huṃ ka va ca gaḥ (translation
courtesy of Dr Bernd Jesse)

Detail of sutra calligraphy

14

## STORAGE BOX FOR THE LOTUS SUTRA
4.5 x 5.0 x 28.0 cm.
Unsigned
Nineteenth century

This box is made from a rare hardwood covered in clear lacquer. The gold lacquer inscription indicates that it was intended to contain the *Fumonbon*, Chapter 25 of the *Hokkekyō* [Lotus Sutra]. Along the right side of the cover is the name *Kōmyō Kōgō* [Empress Kōmyō, 701-60]. The consort of the Emperor Shōmu, like her husband she played a vital role in the establishment of the Buddhist faith in Japan. The interior of the lid is decorated with the favorite lacquer motif of chrysanthemum blossoms floating down a stream. First translated from Sanskrit into Chinese during the third century AD, the Lotus Sutra relates the final sermon of the Buddha before his entry into nirvana. It is perhaps the most important text of East Asian Buddhism.

**Reference:**
Miner, Earl, Odagiri, Hiroko, and Morrell, Robert E., *The Princeton Companion to Classical Japanese Literature* (Princeton, 1985), 383 (*s.v.* 'Kannongyō').

## 15

## MINIATURE WRITING-BOX

3.0 x 10.0 x 12.0 cm.
The storage box signed *urushi-shō Hyōkan* [lacquerworker Hyōkan],
with a seal *urushi-shō Oka Hyōkan* [lacquerworker Oka Hyōkan], and
*maki-e-shi Mitsutaka* [*maki-e* master Mitsutaka], with a seal *Mitsutaka*
Twentieth century

The subject-matter of this box is based on poem by the daughter
of the courtier Saki no dainagon Saneaki, number 1636 in the
*Fūgawakashū*, an Imperial anthology of the mid-fourteenth century:

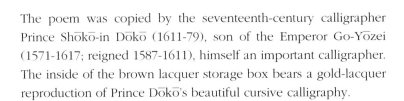

*Asagarasu*
*koe suru mori no*
*kozue shimo*
*tsuki wa yofukaki*
*ariake no kage*

Even at daybreak
when the squawks of crows are heard
from the branches of the wood
the moon casts its pale shadows
as if it were still night.

The poem was copied by the seventeenth-century calligrapher
Prince Shōkō-in Dōkō (1611-79), son of the Emperor Go-Yōzei
(1571-1617; reigned 1587-1611), himself an important calligrapher.
The inside of the brown lacquer storage box bears a gold-lacquer
reproduction of Prince Dōkō's beautiful cursive calligraphy.

From the style of the signature Hyōkan would appear to be in the
line of lacquer artists founded by Kimura Hyōsai (1817-85) of Kyoto,
whose successors used the character *Hyō* in their names.

**Reference:**

Araki Tadasu, *Dai Nihon shoga meika taikan* [A dictionary of Japanese
    painters and calligraphers] (Tokyo, 1934), vol. 2, 2193.
Gōke, T., Hutt, J. and Wrangham, E. A., *Meiji no Takara, Treasures of
    Imperial Japan, Lacquer* (London, 1995), cat. no. 28.
Wrangham, E. A., *The Index of Inrō Artists* (Harehope, Northumberland,
    1995), 84 (*s.v.* 'Hyōsai I and II').

16

## WRITING-BOX
4.5 x 22.0 x 24.0 cm.
Unsigned
Early twentieth century

Several gifted lacquer artists of the nineteenth and twentieth centuries have taken up the challenge of creating delicate, representational feather designs. The technique used for the depiction of feathers on this box is extremely sophisticated and accounts for their fragile beauty. The web of the feather is done in *togidashi-e* technique (see page 9), where the completed design is covered over with several layers of lacquer which are then polished flat until the design reappears, flush with the newly created ground. The down at the base of the feather is in the slightly raised *takamaki-e* technique, as is the quill. A further feather decorates the small silver *suiteki* [container used to hold water for mixing with the ink on the ink-stone]. Both the *suiteki* (metal artist: James Kelso) and the ink-stone (lacquer artist: Sadae Walters) are contemporary replacements.

**Reference:**
Gōke, Tadaomi, Hutt, Julia, and Wrangham, E. A., *Meiji no Takara, Treasures of Imperial Japan, Lacquer* (London, 1995), cat. nos. 29, 32.

Details of feathers

17

## WRITING-BOX AND DOCUMENT-BOX

Writing-box: 6.0 x 27.0 x 29.0 cm.
Document-box: 16.4 x 37.0 x 45.0 cm.
Signed under the ink-stone *Hokkyō Kōrin* with a seal *Hōshuku*
Eighteenth century

These boxes illustrate the subject of a No play which describes a legendary episode in the life of the Tang-dynasty Chinese poet Bo Juyi (772-847, usually called Haku Rakuten in Japanese), whose verses had an immense influence on early Japanese literature. An apocryphal tradition relates that Haku Rakuten was sent to Japan by the Emperor of China to 'subdue' Japan with his art. In the No play, Haku arrives at the coast of Bizen Province where he meets two Japanese fishermen, one of whom is in reality the god of Japanese poetry, Sumiyoshi Myōjin. In the second scene Sumiyoshi Myōjin reveals his identity and summons the other gods. In the ensuing dance-scene, the wind from the gods' sleeves blows the foreign poet back to China. Haku Rakuten appears on the document-box and Sumiyoshi Myōjin is the subject of the writing-box.

The same design appears on a set of boxes in a Japanese private collection and has its origins in two screens by Ogata Kōrin (1658-1716), one of them in the Nezu Institute of Fine Arts, Tokyo. It was later reproduced in *Kōrin hyakuzu* (see catalog number 20). The numerous heavy lead inlays representing the islands of the Inland Sea, the bold use of shell and the form of the waves are all features of Kōrin's lacquer style. The design of waves and islands is continued inside the box.

**Reference:**

Joly, Henri L. and Tomita, Kumasaku, *Japanese Art and Handicraft, Loan Exhibition Held in Aid of the British Red Cross* (London, 1916), lacquer no. 21 (pl.LXIV).

Link, Howard A., *Exquisite Visions: Rimpa Paintings from Japan* (exhibition catalog by Tōru Shimbo, Honolulu Academy of Arts, 1980; Honolulu, 1980), cat. no. 17.

Waley, Arthur, *The Nō Plays of Japan* (London, 1921), 248-57.

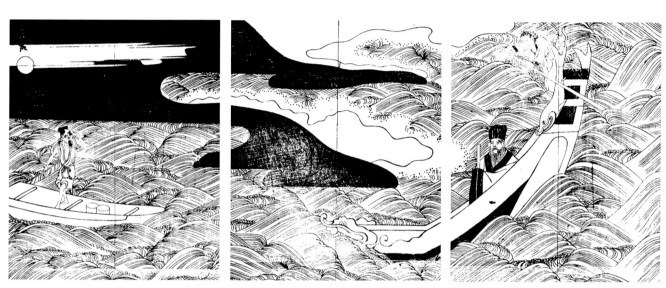

Figure 17a
Woodblock printed designs from the *Kōrin hyakuzu* [One hundred designs by Kōrin] published in 1815 and 1826 by Sakai Hōitsu.

Six-panel folding screen; color on gold-leaf paper;
148 x 361 cm.
Signed *Hokkyō Kōrin,*
Seal: *Masatoki.*
From a private collection, Tokyo, reprinted from *Rimpa Paintings from Japan* (Honolulu, 1980).

18

**WRITING-BOX**
4.8 x 19.2 x 25.9 cm.
Signed *Hokkyō Kōrin*
Eighteenth century

The box is constructed from a single slab of paulownia wood, the top and bottom of the box being formed by the separation of natural cleavage lines in the wood. The design of the deer, the *torii* [shrine archway] and the trees suggests the Kasuga Shrine in Nara. Silver staples have been applied to simulate repairs and reinforcements.

For Ogata Kōrin, see also catalog number 17.

**Published:**
Pekarik, Andrew J., *Japanese Lacquer, 1600-1900: Selections from the Charles A. Greenfield Collection* (exhibition catalog, New York, Metropolitan Museum of Art, September 4-October 19, 1980; New York, 1980), fig. 67 (cat. no. 55).

19

## WRITING-BOX

5.1 x 21.4 x 29.0 cm.
Signed *Tsuchida Sōetsu* with a *kaō* [monogram]
Eighteenth century

A group of four deer, two of them calling with their heads raised, is depicted in lead on the lid of this writing-box. The box includes a plain, square water-dropper of the kind traditionally associated with lacquers in the style of Ogata Kōrin (1658-1716). Tsuchida Sōetsu, whose signature appears on the reverse of the lid alongside a design of maple-leaves and a dragonfly, is believed to have lived from 1660 to 1745 and to have followed the style initiated by Kōrin and his predecessor Hon'ami Kōetsu (1558-1637). He thus anticipated the more widespread revival of the so-called Rimpa style that took place in the early nineteenth century.

**Reference:**

Wrangham, E. A., 'The Return of Rimpa', in Gōke, Tadaomi, Hutt, Julia, and Wrangham, E. A., *Meiji no Takara, Treasures of Imperial Japan, Lacquer* (London, 1995), vol. 1, (56-65), 62-4.

20

**WRITING-BOX**
2.8 x 15.2 x 16.5 cm.
Signed *Jisei*
Nineteenth century

Matsushima is an archipelago of more than 260 sparsely pine-clad islands in a bay in north-eastern Japan well known for its active waves. One of the 'Three Chief Sights' of Japan, it was celebrated in screen paintings by Ogata Kōrin (1658-1716), one of the most important artists in Japan's history (see catalog numbers 17-19).

The wave design on this writing-box was accomplished by the *seigaiha* [combed wave] technique (see catalog numbers 7, 67), which was revived by Shibata Zeshin and his pupil Ikeda Taishin (1825-1903). While the waves on this box appear rougher and less delicate than the combing characteristic of Zeshin, they are, in fact, accurate representations of the waves depicted by Kōrin, as recorded in *Kōrin hyakuzu* [One hundred designs by Kōrin], a woodblock-printed book published in 1815 and 1826 during the early nineteenth-century revival of his style.

Nothing is known of the artist who signed this piece.

Woodblock printed designs from the *Kōrin hyakuzu* [One hundred designs by Kōrin] published in 1815 and 1826 by Sakai Hōitsu.

## 21

**STORAGE CABINET**
22.0 x 19.5 x 30.0 cm.
Signed *Ritsuō* with a seal *Kan*
Eighteenth century

Inlaid upon the shell background of this box are objects which would be present on the study table of a Chinese or Japanese scholar. These include ink-cakes, an ink-stone and a brush, all requisite for the East Asian art of calligraphy, as well as objects of antiquarian interest such as examples of Chinese Han-dynasty (BC 206-220 AD) coins, a bronze seal with a *shishi* [temple lion], and a bronze mirror. The handle of the brush has the appearance of *tsuishu* [carved red lacquer] and the lacquer ink-cakes are so realistic as to suggest that the true objects have been placed on the box. Chinese scholars' articles were among the favorite subjects of Ogawa Haritsu (Ritsuō, 1663-1747, see catalog numbers 22-7), whose name and seal (*Kan*) appear on an ink-cake on the rear panel of the box. The designs of some of the other ink-cakes are taken from the *Fangshi mopu* (see catalog numbers 22, 24-5).

Detail of lacquer ink cake with tortoise.

Lacquer ink cake signed Ritsuo, sealed Kan.

Block print of tortoise design from the *Fangshi mopu*.

Detail of a lacquer ink stick in the shape of an ancient coin.

## 22

**WRITING-BOX**
2.3 x 20.4 x 24.0 cm.
Signed *Kyōho mizunoe-tatsu Ritsuō* [Ritsuō in the *mizunoe-tatsu* [1712]
year of Kyōho], with a seal *Kan*
1712

The writing-box is of a rough open-grained wood with pottery and
ivory inlaid sea-shells. Beads of water are represented by small
metallic circles inset with stained ivory. Green lacquer seaweed is
scattered about. The inside of the box is in red lacquer. On the
underside of the lid is a silver-lacquered twenty-character celebra-
tion of spring in Chinese seal script. There are several extant boxes
with sea-shell motifs signed by Ritsuō (see catalog numbers 21,
23-7) and it has been suggested that these may owe their origin to
a design entitled *Xuanhai xiaochen* [The precious fruits of the
mysterious sea] which is found in two Chinese books of ink-cake
designs, the *Fangshi mopu* (see catalog numbers 21, 24-5) and the
*Chengshi moyuan* (1606).

**Published:**

Joly, Henri L. and Tomita, Kumasaku, *Japanese Art and Handicraft, Loan
    Exhibition Held in Aid of the British Red Cross* (London, 1916), cat. no.
    37 (p. 60), pl. LXI.

**Reference:**

Earle, Joe (ed.), *The Toshiba Gallery: Japanese Art and Design* [in the
    Victoria and Albert Museum] (London, 1986), cat. no. 37.
Kyoto National Museum, *Ritsuō saiku* [Inlaid lacquerwork by Ritsuō]
    (Kyoto, 1992), cat. no. 17.
Yonemura, Ann, *Japanese Lacquer* [in the Freer Gallery of Art] (Washington
    DC, 1979), 84.

23

## MEDICINE-CASE IN THREE SECTIONS

7.5 x 7.5 x 2.6 cm.

Signed *Kyōho hinoe-saru shūjitsu Ritsuō sei* [made by Ritsuō on an autumn day in the *hinoe-saru* year [1716] of the Kyōho era], with a seal *Kan*

1716

This *inrō* is fitted with a sheath in the form of a chipped old ink-cake created from carved black lacquer. A light application of gold lacquer highlights the design of a *hōō* [phoenix]. The reverse is set with a ceramic plaque depicting a stylized white dragon with gold lacquer highlights on a green ground. This is identical to a plaque that appears on a simulated ink-cake on the cover of a writing-box by Ogawa Haritsu (see catalog numbers 21-2, 24-7) in Tokyo National Museum, dated 1720. Inside the sheath is a simple three-case *inrō* of black lacquer on a leather base. This may be the oldest dated *inrō* of the sheath type.

Like many other *inrō* in the collection, this one is fitted with a silk cord threaded onto an *ojime* [tighening bead] and netsuke [toggle].

*Ojime*: Lacquer.

Netsuke: Ebony, simulating an ink-stick with a dragon on one side and calligraphy on the reverse, with a seal *Kan*.

**Published:**

Pekarik, Andrew J., *Japanese Lacquer, 1600-1900: Selections from the Charles A. Greenfield Collection* (exhibition catalog, New York, Metropolitan Museum of Art, September 4-October 19, 1980; New York, 1980), pl. 15 (cat. no. 64).

**Reference:**

Kyoto National Museum, *Ritsuō saiku* [Inlaid lacquerwork by Ritsuō] (Kyoto, 1992), cat. no. 4.

Yonemura, Ann, *Japanese Lacquer* [in the Freer Gallery of Art] (Washington DC, 1979), 76-85.

## 24

## MEDICINE-CASE

16.5 x 3.8 x 2.2 cm.
With a seal *Urushi Setsuzan* [lacquer by Setsuzan]
Nineteenth century

This *inrō* is in the form of a Chinese ink-stick. Along the lower right border of the *inrō* is the Chinese signature *Fangshi Jianyuan* with a seal *Jianyuan*. This is an alternative name for Fang Yulu, a famous Chinese maker of ink (*fl. c.* 1570-1619) who compiled an important illustrated catalog of designs for ink-cakes, the *Fangshi mopu*, the first edition of which was published *c.* 1588. It is thought that this book was first imported to Japan in the early eighteenth century, when a copy entered the library of Tsugaru Nobutoshi (1669-1746), a *daimyō* [feudal lord] for whom Ogawa Haritsu (see catalog numbers 21-3, 25-7) worked from 1723. To the right of the main design is a six-character Chinese date-inscription *Manreki kinoto-tori shunjitsu* [a spring day in the *yiyou* year [1585] of the Wanli era]. At the top of the *inrō* is another inscription of unknown origin which may read *your servant subdues the warlike barbarians*. This is presumably an allusion to the outlandish long-legged wine-drinking foreigners featured on both sides of the *inrō*. The early years of the eighteenth century saw a revival of interest in the exotic, exemplified by the illustrations of weird and wonderful foreign beings assembled by the doctor and scholar Terajima Ryōan for his encyclopedia *Wakan sansai zue*, based on a Chinese original. After this time 'long-legs' (*ashinaga*) are often seen in both netsuke and *inrō*.

An oval seal to the right of the inscription about the barbarians reads *urushi Setsuzan* [lacquer by Setsuzan]. Setsuzan (also read Sessan) is a name apparently used by the famous lacquerer Hara Yōyūsai (1772-1845/6, see catalog number 12) or one of his successors, although some authorities do not list it.

For a further discussion of this *inrō*, see page 13.

**Reference:**

Goodrich, L. Carrington, *Dictionary of Ming Biography* (New York and London, 1976), vol. 1, 438-9.

Takao Yō, 'Kinsei makie-shi meikan 4 [A list of Edo- and Meiji-period *maki-e* artists, part 4]', *Rokushō*, 20 (1996), (104-10), 105-6.

Terajima, Ryōan, *Wakan sansai zue* [Illustrated Japanese-Chinese encyclopedia of the three realms] (Tokyo, 1970; original edn. Osaka, 1716), 228.

Wrangham, E. A., *The Index of Inrō Artists* (Harehope, Northumberland, 1995), 340.

Yonemura, Ann, *Japanese Lacquer* [in the Freer Gallery of Art] (Washington DC, 1979), 74-85.

25

## INCENSE-BOX

2.0 x 4.8 x 5.4 cm.
Signed *Tsuchinoe-saru risshun Ritsuō sei* [made by Ritsuō on the first
day of spring in the *tsuchinoe-saru* year] with a seal *Kan.*
Eighteenth or nineteenth century

The large characters in the center of the reverse read *Kyūkō* [nine
tributes], a term used to refer to a richly caparisoned elephant
bearing a boat-shaped offering vessel on its back. This motif, a
favorite of Ritsuō's, derived from two Chinese Ming-dynasty albums
of ink-cake design, *Fangshi mopu* and *Chengshi moyuan* (see
catalog numbers 21-2, 24). The elephant is the attribute of the
bodhisattva Fugen, a divine being who renounced entry into
nirvana in order to relieve the sufferings of mankind. On this
incense-box the elephant is replaced by a lion, the attribute of
Monju, the bodhisattva of wisdom. This departure from Haritsu's
usual iconography, coupled with the unusual form of the date,
which omits the name of the reign-period, Kyōho, suggests that this
may be an example of the nineteenth-century revival of the Haritsu
style.

**Reference:**
Davey, Neil K., and Tripp, Susan, *The Garrett Collection, Japanese Art:
    Lacquer, Inrō, Netsuke* (London, 1993), cat. no. 12.
Tokugawa Art Museum, *Koboku* [Old carbon ink sticks in the Tokugawa
    Art Museum] (Kyoto, 1991), cat. no. 114, an ink stick with lion design
    by Wu Shenbo (Shengyang).
Gōke, Tadaomi, Hutt, Julia, and Wrangham, E. A., *Meiji no Takara,
    Treasures of Imperial Japan, Lacquer* (London, 1995), cat. no. 48
Kyoto National Museum, *Ritsuō saiku* [Inlaid lacquerwork by Ritsuō]
    (Kyoto, 1992), 68.

## 26

## BOX

5.2 x 16.0 x 20.7 cm.
Sealed *Tenrokudō* and *Kenkoku kinsei* [respectfully made by Kenkoku]
Parts of the box probably seventeenth or early eighteenth century, the exterior decoration
*circa* 1875-85

An inset circular panel on the lid of the box shows Bodhidharma (Daruma, see catalog number 27 and 32) in lacquered pottery on a gold leaf background. He is depicted with non-Japanese facial features, a gold ear-ring, and blue eyes, in a style traditionally attributed to the painter Soga Jasoku (*d.* 1483) and his contemporaries. One of the two red lacquer seals on the outside of this box indicates that the ceramic decoration is by Miura Ken'ya I (1825-89), who used the art-name Tenrokudō. Ken'ya was both a gifted potter in the tradition founded by the great Ogata Kenzan (1663-1743) and a pioneering technologist who worked on the first Japanese steamboat and later produced the first Western-style bricks in Japan. According to one tradition he only copied the style of Ogawa Haritsu (Ritsuō, see catalog numbers 21-5, 27), as here, until the early Meiji period. The other seal, *Kenkoku*, is that of Itō Sadabumi (or Teibun) Kenkoku (*b.*1853), a lacquer technician, restorer and educator who around the beginning of the Meiji period (according to one authority, in the seventh year of Meiji, 1874) received instruction in pottery from Ken'ya in return for teaching him lacquering.

The interior is decorated with lotus-leaves in gold and silver lacquer on a thin black lacquer ground that has turned a brownish color with age, and the whole box shows signs of considerable reworking and repair, suggesting that the two artists converted an old piece in order to get the antique look required for the Ritsuō style.

For a further discussion of this box, see page 13.

### Published:

Burlington Fine Arts Club, *Exhibition of Japanese Lacquer and Metal Work* (London, 1894), table
    case X, no. 1.
Gilbertson, E., *et al., A Japanese Collection Made by Michael Tomkinson* (London, 1898), lacquer
    no. 471 (plate facing p. 44).

### Reference:

Araki Tadasu, *Dai Nihon shoga meika taikan* [A dictionary of Japanese painters and calligraphers]
    (Tokyo, 1934), vol. 2, pl. 1.
Takeuchi Kyūichi, 'Ritsuō seisaku no kōkeisha [The inheritors of the Ritsuō style]', *Shoga kottō
    zasshi* [Painting and antiques magazine] (Apr. 1916), 25-9.
Tokyo National Research Institute of Cultural Properties, *Naikoku kangyō hakurankai bijutsuhin
    shuppin mokuroku* [Catalogs of objects exhibited at the National Industrial Expositions] (Tokyo,
    1996), 248 (no. 575).
Tsuda Noritake, untitled manuscript known as the 'Tsuda manuscript' (Tokyo, 1908) [privately
    produced English translation, 1986].
Wrangham, E. A., *The Index of Inrō Artists* (Harehope, Northumberland, 1995), 125, 152, 286.

Seals reading
*Tenrokudō* and
*Kenkoku kinsei*
[respectfully
made by
Kenkoku].

Detail from
inside of box
revealing
fallen lotus
petals

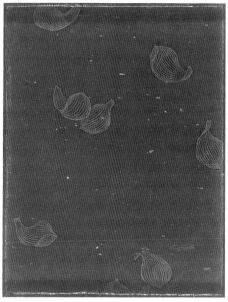

## 27

## BOX

6.0 x 20.0 x 28.0 cm.
Signed *Gyōnen hachijūichi-ō Muchūan zō* [made by Muchūan, an old man of eighty-one]
with a red and white pottery seal *Kan*
Nineteenth century

On this box Bodhidharma (Daruma, see catalog numbers 26 and 32) is depicted in red
and brown lacquers, in contrast to the ceramic inlay of the Ken'ya box. His massive
form contrasts with the tiny ceramic incense-burner on a table to his right as he looks
out from a hole broken through the rotting wooden wall of a temple. The interior of
the lid shows a rat and a *hossu* [Buddhist priest's fly whisk], a symbol of religious
leadership; another rat squats in an opening in a wall. In the interior of the base of the
box is a red-lacquered *mokugyo* [temple gong in the shape of a fish] with its hammer
and a *nyoi* [cloud-sceptre] alongside.

The name *Muchūan* and the seal *Kan* were used by Ogawa Haritsu (see catalog
numbers 21-6), but the style and technique, including the use of *togidashi-e* (see page
9), are uncharacteristic of Ritsuō and the box is more likely to be the work of a
nineteenth-century artist.

### Published:

Gilbertson, E., *et al., A Japanese Collection Made by Michael Tomkinson* (London, 1898), lacquer
no. 643.

Details of the rats appearing on the inside of
the lid

Design of a lotus plant in the *togidashi-e*
technique on the bottom of the box

## 28

**MEDICINE-CASE IN FOUR SECTIONS**
6.0 x 5.0 x 2.2 cm.
Unsigned
Eighteenth or nineteenth century

Chinese coins of the Dading and Taiping eras (see catalog number 29) appear on a lacquer background imitating rotting wood. Another coin has transformed itself into a butterfly, each wing made of one half of the coin, which bears the first character of the Xuande era (1426-36) and the character *bao* [treasure] often seen on Chinese and Japanese money. The top and bottom are inscribed in Chinese seal script with a seven-character couplet from a Chinese poem.

*Ojime* [bead]: Coral.

Netsuke: Lacquered wood; a Chinese coin.

**Reference:**
Kyoto National Museum, *Ritsuō saiku* [Inlaid lacquerwork by Ritsuō] (Kyoto, 1992), cat. no. 25.

*29*

## MEDICINE-CASE IN FOUR SECTIONS
7.3 x 3.3 x 3.5 cm.
Signed *Hanzan*
Mid-eighteenth century

The era-names on the Chinese coins mimicked on this *inrō* include Dading (555-62 and 1161-89), Taiping (several different eras from the third to the eleventh century), and Kangxi (1662-1722).

Mochizuki Hanzan took the art name Haritsu II in honor of his master Ogawa Haritsu (see catalog numbers 21-7) and shared his predilection for antiquarian Chinese subjects.

**Reference:**
Takao Yō, 'Kinsei makie-shi meikan 4 [A list of Edo- and Meiji-period *maki-e* artists, part 4]', *Rokushō*, 20 (1996), (104-10), 108.
Wrangham, E. A., *The Index of Inrō Artists* (Harehope, Northumberland, 1995), 67.

## 30

**MEDICINE-CASE IN FOUR SECTIONS**
8.7 x 5.3 x 3.0 cm.
Signed *Mizutani Shūtōho*
Late eighteenth-nineteenth century

Mizutani Shūtōho was an artist, usually thought to have been active in the mid-eighteenth century, whose work was highly influenced by Ogawa Haritsu (see catalog numbers 21-7).

One of the coins depicted on this *inrō* bears the reign-name of the Chinese Emperor Jiaqing (reigned 1796-1820) providing evidence that either Shūtōho or an imitator was active at the very end of the century, if not somewhat later.

**Reference:**
Takao Yō, 'Kinsei makie-shi meikan 4 [A list of Edo- and Meiji-period *maki-e* artists, part 4]', *Rokushō*, 20 (1996), (104-10), 107.
Wrangham, E. A., *The Index of Inrō Artists* (Harehope, Northumberland, 1995), 268.

31

## INCENSE-BOX

2.2 x 6.6 x 6.6 cm.
Inscribed *Kōtei kyūzui* [the Yellow Emperor's auspicious palace]
Signed in seal form *Masayuki*
Nineteenth century

This incense-box in the manner of Ogawa Haritsu (see catalog numbers 21-7) is fashioned in the form of an old ink-cake showing the monk Sanzō Hōshi or Genjō (in Chinese, Xuanzang, 596-664) with the monkey which helped him perform 108 deeds as a test of his holiness on his travels from China to India. An important Buddhist philosopher of the idealist 'Consciousness-Only' school, after his death Xuanzang rapidly became the subject of a whole cycle of fantastic legends which were later immortalized in the sixteenth-century novel translated by Arthur Waley as *Monkey*.

The reverse also follows Haritsu's style in featuring a four-character inscription in archaic style which is apparently unconnected to the Sanzō Hōshi story. The inside shows the moon above waves; this may be intended as a reference to the moon-palace, the dwelling of the Yellow Emperor.

The only recorded lacquerer who signed his name *Masayuki* (also read *Seishi*) was the sixth master of the Yamamoto Shunshō line (1774-1831). However, the same characters are also seen on many late Edo- (1615-1868) and Meiji-period (1868-1912) works of art in a variety of media, making to difficult to assign this box to any particular artist.

**Reference:**
Chan, Wing-Tsit, *A Source Book in Chinese Philosophy* (Princeton, 1963), 370.
Wrangham, E. A., *The Index of Inro Artists* (Harehope, Northumberland, 1995), 228 (*s.v.* 'Seishi').
Wu, Cheng-en, *Monkey*, trans. Arthur Waley, London, 1942.

## 32

**MEDICINE-CASE**
8.0 x 5.5 x 3.0 cm.
Signed *Tōkō* with a *kaō* [monogram]
Nineteenth century

Bodhidharma, or Daruma (see catalog numbers 26-7), is the patriarch who introduced Chan (*Zen*) Buddhism to China in the sixth century. He is the physical embodiment of the doctrine of contemplation and meditation. On the reverse of the sheath of this *inrō* are lotus plants, representing purity. A cicada sits on the stem of the flower, symbolizing the religious phenomenon of reincarnation.

*Ojime* [bead]: Smoky quartz.

Netsuke: Wood; Daruma, signed *Tōkoku*

**Signature published:**
Wrangham, E. A., *The Index of Inrō Artists* (Harehope, Northumberland, 1995), 294.

## 33

**STORAGE-BOX FOR MEDICINE-CASES**
32.5 x 41.0 x 30.0 cm.
Unsigned
Nineteenth century

The hare has long played an important part in Japanese folklore, making an appearance in the early historical chronicle, *Kojiki* [Record of ancient matters], completed in AD 712. The Sanskrit word for 'hare' is *cacadharas* [one who carries the moon] and the association between hare and moon has always been strong in Japan and other parts of Asia. On this light-hearted but technically refined example, a storage-box for *inrō*, the hare and moon are shown with autumn plants including chrysanthemums and *hagi* [bush-clover], alluding to the moon-viewing ceremony that takes place on the fifteenth day of the eighth lunar month, corresponding roughly to late September.

The cabinet is fitted with five drawers for *inrō* and netsuke.

### Reference:
Jahss, Melvin and Betty, *Inrō, and Other Miniature Forms of Japanese Lacquer Art* (London, 1971), 334-5.
Joly, Henri L., *Legend in Japanese Art* (London, 1908), 194-7.
Williams, C. A. S., *Outlines of Chinese Symbolism and Art Motives* (Rutland, Vermont, 1974; original edn. Shanghai, 1941), 220, 278.

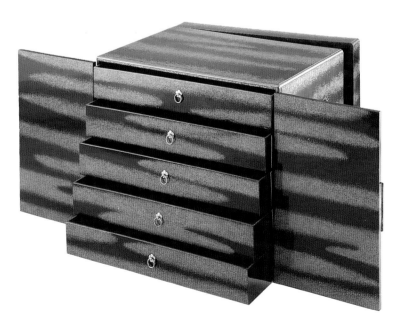

34

**MEDICINE-CASE IN ONE SECTION**
8.3 x 4.5 x 2.7 cm.
Unsigned
Eighteenth century

The design of phoenixes on this *inrō* is executed in fine silver and gold wire. Above one phoenix, in a cartouche, is the word *MAAN* (with the *N* backwards) and on the reverse side is *ZON*. These are the Dutch words for 'moon' and 'sun'. The *inrō* reflects the eighteenth-century Japanese taste for objects made from exotic materials or incorporating foreign designs. It contains a hinged sandalwood insert enclosing a miniature sculpture of Christ and a representation of the Madonna and Child. These were probably added by a later owner.

*Ojime* [bead]: A metal cross.

Netsuke: Blue and white porcelain; a three-masted square-rigged European ship, signed *Shonzui.*

**Reference:**
Glendining and Co., auction catalog of the W. L. Behrens Collection [by H. L. Joly], pt. ii. Lacquer and Inro (London, 1914), 20 (no. 138), pl. XVII.

## 35

### MEDICINE-CASE IN ONE SECTION

4.1 x 7.7 x 3.3 cm.
Signed *Fujin saku* [made by Fujin]
Nineteenth century

The case is decorated with birds among scrolling vines, with a silver clasp depicting dragons, and false silver hinges. The leaves and flowers are of colored lacquer within gold borders applied in a manner similar to the way in which cloisonné enamels are delimited by inlaid wires. The birds are highlighted in red lacquer, *nashiji* [gold flakes] and *aogai nashiji* [crushed mother of pearl]. The whole design has a somewhat foreign appearance, recalling the embossed leather patterns reproduced by Inaba Tsūryū in *Sōken Kishō* (1781).

Fujin [literally 'inexhaustible'] is supposed to be the name of a noted seventeenth-century lacquerer who worked for the wealthy Maeda family in Kaga province. The use of his name here is probably an honorific tribute rather than an attempt to deceive.

*Ojime* [bead]: *Shibuichi* [copper and silver alloy]; flying birds.

Netsuke: *Shakudō* (see catalog number 64); chrysanthemums and scrolling vines.

**Reference:**

Inaba Tsūryū Shin'emon, *Sōken Kishō* [Strange and wonderful sword-fittings], vol. 6 (partly reproduced in Arakawa Hirokazu, *The Gō Collection of Netsuke* (Tokyo, 1983); Osaka, 1781).

Wrangham, E. A., *The Index of Inrō Artists* (Harehope, Northumberland, 1995), 52.

36

## PIPE-CASE

21.5 x 3.3 cm.
Signed *Hisamine*
Nineteenth century

This *kiseruzutsu* [pipecase] of lacquered leather and ivory depicts a Dutchman and his dog. The foreigner is well dressed in eighteenth-century costume. Tobacco was introduced to Japan by the Portuguese in the mid-sixteenth century. It was banned as a fire hazard in 1611, but the law was repealed in 1716.

Nothing is known of this artist.

**Reference:**
Ducros, Alain, *Netsuke & Sagemono 2* (Granges-les-Valence, 1987), 165-9.

37

## MEDICINE-CASE IN FOUR SECTIONS

9.7 x 5.4 x 2.8 cm.

Signed *Kansai*, with a red *kaō* [monogram]

Nineteenth century

During the Edo period (1615-1868), the reigning shogun required each of the *daimyō* [feudal lords] to visit Edo (now Tokyo) every year with his entourage of samurai. The procession was headed by a *yakko* [retainer] carrying a staff topped with horsehair. The *yakko* announced the arrival of the *daimyō* and the peasantry were required to bow down and not lift their heads, under penalty of death. The *yakko* were frequently the butt of satire.

On this *inrō* a *yakko* sits under a flowering cherry-tree, the petals floating down around him, drinking from a red lacquer sake cup. In his drunken state he dreams of characters which appeared in a popular art form associated with the town of Ōtsu. *Ōtsu-e* [Ōtsu pictures] were primitive paintings, usually with popular Buddhist imagery, produced for pilgrims passing through the town. The *Ōtsu-e* subjects depicted here are: the longevity god Jurōjin, the Wistaria Maiden, a cat playing a *samisen* [three-stringed instrument] and a monkey.

The most unusual feature of the technique employed for this *inrō* is the *yamimaki-e* [black-on-black] technique which depicts the dream. The dream is subtle and almost invisible in natural light, but becomes apparent when brightly illuminated.

The first of the two principal Koma Kansai died in 1792 and his successor Kansai II lived from 1767 to 1835. He was the lacquer master of Shibata Zeshin (1807-91, see catalog numbers 67-82) who also enjoyed using the *yamimaki-e* technique.

*Ojime* [bead]: Serpentine.

Netsuke: ivory; a *baku*. The *baku* is a mythological creature with an elephant's trunk and tusks, a rhinoceros's eyes, the body of a lion, the tail of an ox and the feet of a tiger. The *baku* feeds on bad dreams, promoting restful sleep.

**Reference:**

Michener, James A., 'In the Village of Otsu' in *The Floating World* (Honolulu, 1983; original edn. New York, 1954), ch. 1.

**38**

## MEDICINE-CASE IN THREE SECTIONS
6.5 x 5.0 x 1.7 cm.
Unsigned
Eighteenth-early nineteenth century

This *inrō* shows the Seven Sages of the Bamboo Grove, a group of third-century poets and literati who gathered for the purpose of intellectual conviviality. They are Genseki (in Chinese, Yuan Ji), expert at the flute and zither; Keikō (Ji Kang), drummer, painter and calligrapher; Santō (Shan Tao), patron of rising talent who could make himself invisible; Shōshū (Xiang Xiu), expert on the Daoist classics normally shown holding a scroll; Ryūrei (Liu Ling), devoted to pleasure and usually carrying a book; Genkan (Yuan Xian), another musician; and Ōjū (Wang Rong), lover of plums.

*Ojime* [bead]: Pearl.

**Reference:**

Jahss, Melvin and Betty, *Inrō, and Other Miniature Forms of Japanese Lacquer Art* (London, 1971), 297.

Tsang, Gerard, and Moss, Hugh, 'Scholar, Sage and Monk in Chinese Art: In Pursuit of the Absolute', in Oriental Ceramic Society of Hong Kong, *Arts from the Scholar's Studio* (exhibition catalog, Hong Kong, Fung Ping Shan Museum, October 24-December 13, 1986; Hong Kong, 1986).

39

## MEDICINE-CASE IN THREE SECTIONS
6.4 x 6.4 x 2.2 cm.
Signed *Shumpōsai saku* [made by Shumpōsai]
Nineteenth century

The images of these two popular immortals of the Daoist pantheon, Tekkai Sennin and Gama Sennin, are interpretations of classic paintings by the fourteenth-century Chinese master, Yan Hui; similar designs are seen on *inrō* by other artists such as Yamada Jōkasai, Shumpōsai and members of the Koma school. The immortals' Chinese names are Xiama or Liu Hai (in Japanese, Gama) and Tieguai (Tekkai). Gama Sennin is depicted with a three-legged toad on his shoulder. On the reverse side is Tekkai Sennin who is shown blowing his spirit toward heaven. One legend describes Tekkai's spirit as having left his body in order to ascend to heaven to have discourse with the founder of Daoism, Laozi. Upon the spirit's return, Tekkai's body could not be found and so it entered the body of a lame beggar who had previously died. Tekkai's spirit was thereafter forced to live in this humble beggar's body. For a different version of Tekkai's story, see catalog number 40.

*Ojime* [bead]: Silver metal cocoon with emerging moth.

**Reference:**

Carpenter, Janet, 'The Immortals of Taoism', in Addiss, Stephen (ed.), *Japanese Ghosts and Demons: Art of the Supernatural* (exhibition catalog, June 13-September 1, 1985; New York and Lawrence, Kansas, 1985), 57-65.

Joly, Henri L., *Legend in Japanese Art* (London, 1908), 159, 527.

Kress, Heinz, 'Inro Motifs, Part I', *Netsuke Kenkyukai Journal*, 14/2 (Summer 1994), 24-37 (figs. 18-25).

Tsuji, Nobuo, *Playfulness in Japanese Art* (The Franklin D. Murphy lectures, Spencer Museum of Art, University of Kansas, 1986; Lawrence, Kansas, 1986), 31-4.

Wrangham, E. A., *The Index of Inrō Artists* (Harehope, Northumberland, 1995), 263-4.

Portraits of Gama Sennin and Tekkai Sennin by Chinese artist Yan Hui (1360-1368),
Collection of the Chionji Temple, Kyoto. Illustrated in 'A Gallery of Japanese and Chinese Paintings', *Kokka*, 1908, figure XXVI.

40

## MEDICINE-CASE IN FOUR SECTIONS
8.5 x 6.0 x 2.0 cm.
Signed *Koma Kyūhaku saku* [made by Koma Kyūhaku]
Late eighteenth-early nineteenth century

Tekkai Sennin (the Chinese Immortal Li Tieguai, 'Iron-Crutch Li') is shown exhaling his spirit. One of the most popular among the large number of semi-mythical Chinese beings re-introduced to Japan from the Asian continent in the sixteenth and seventeenth centuries, Tekkai was, according to one legend, a Daoist sage whose body was accidentally burnt by his servant after his death. As a result, his soul was forced to inhabit the body of an emaciated beggar. For a slightly different version of this story, see catalog number 39.

For Koma Kyūhaku, see catalog number 51.

### Reference:
Oriental Ceramic Society, *Chinese Ivories from the Shang to the Qing* (exhibition catalog, British Museum, May 24-August 19, 1984; London, 1984), cat. no. 71.

41

## MEDICINE-CASE IN FIVE SECTIONS
10.0 x 4.9 x 2.7 cm.
Signed *Kajikawa* with a red vase-shaped seal
Nineteenth century

Kan'u (in Chinese, Guanyu) was a Chinese hero of the Han dynasty. He died in AD 220 but his fame lived on after him and he was deified as Guandi, God of War, in 1594. He is depicted in Japanese art as a giant of a man holding his long black beard in one hand and a halberd in the other, with a red-pigmented face indicative of his fierce demeanor. This design, which is seen on several other *inrō*, is closely based on the illustrated book *Ehon shahō bukuro*, published in 1720.

The Kajikawa were perhaps the most famous of all Japanese *inrō*-making dynasties and their signature appears on countless pieces, sometimes on its own and sometimes with the addition of an art-name or the family's characteristic seal.

*Ojime*: Ivory.

Netsuke: Ivory; Kan'u with a squire.

### Reference:
Joly, Henri L., *Legend in Japanese Art* (London, 1908), 313-4.

Kress, Heinz, 'Inro Motifs, Part III', *Netsuke Kenkyukai Journal*, 14/4 (Winter 1994), (20-42), 37.

Von Ragué, Beatrix, 'Inro Research: Some Proposed Future Steps', in Bromelle, N. S., and Smith, Perry (eds.), *Urushi* (Proceedings of the Urushi Study Group, June 10-27, 1985, Tokyo; Marina del Rey, Calif., 1988), 23-9.

Wrangham, E. A., *The Index of Inrō Artists* (Harehope, Northumberland, 1995), 107-8.

42

**MEDICINE-CASE IN FOUR SECTIONS**
7.7 x 6.0 x 2.2 cm.
Signed *Koma Kansai saku* [made by Koma Kansai]
Nineteenth century

This *inrō* shows an enormous Buddhist figure, perhaps Hotei, God of Well-Being, smoking his pipe oblivious to six Lilliputians in Chinese dress who cavort through the composition. Tobacco was introduced to Japan by the Portuguese in 1543. The popularity of smoking spread but its use was suppressed by the ruling shogunate during the seventeenth century. The ban was subsequently relaxed and in the nineteenth century, particularly during the Meiji period (1868-1912), smoking paraphernalia became sophisticated art-forms. A lacquer smoking-set is depicted on the reverse side of the *inrō*.

For Koma Kansai, see catalog number 37.

*Ojime* [bead]: Cloisonné enamel.

Netsuke: Vermilion and black Negoro-style lacquer; a *shishi* [temple lion].

**Reference:**
Tanaka, Tomikichi, 'History of Tobacco Pouches', *Netsuke Kenkyukai Journal*, 10/4 (Winter 1990), 8-17.

## 43

### MEDICINE-CASE IN THREE SECTIONS

8.0 x 7.0 x 1.7 cm.
Signed *Kōami Nagataka saku* [made by Kōami Nagataka]
Late eighteenth or nineteenth century

This *inrō* shows a motley crowd of travelers on a ferry-boat. At the bow is a monkey-trainer holding his monkey on a leash while the monkey holds its stand. Among the other passengers are two itinerant *manzai* dancers and a woman with her back turned playing a *samisen* [three-stringed instrument]. On the reverse side are two figures in court dress, a traveler smoking his pipe and a boatman poling the ferry. *Inrō* of this type are often based on much earlier paintings or books showing scenes from everyday life and can give us a rather confused impression of Edo-period costume.

Nagataka (also read Chōkō) was the fifteenth master of the Kōami dynasty of lacquerers, said to have been founded in 1429, and his name appears more often on *inrō* than that of any other Kōami artist. He is believed to have worked in the late eighteenth century, but his signature appears on many later pieces.

*Ojime* [bead]: Ivory; in the form of a climbing monkey.

Netsuke: Wood; a ferry-boat full of passengers, signed *Gyokusō* (*b*.1879).

**Reference:**
Wrangham, E. A., *The Index of Inrō Artists* (Harehope, Northumberland, 1995), 41, 133.
Ueda, Reikichi, *The Netsuke Handbook of Ueda Reikichi* (adapted by Raymond Bushell; Rutland, Vt., and Tokyo, 1961), 225.

## 44

## MEDICINE-CASE IN FOUR SECTIONS
9.0 x 5.0 x 2.4 cm.

Signed *Shunshō* with a seal *Kagemasa* and *Masanobu hitsu* [painted by
Masanobu] with a seal *Masanobu*

Nineteenth century

The signature and seal of the print designer Okumura Masanobu
(1686-1764) appear on the side of this *inrō*, indicating that the
dancing figures are copies of a woodblock print by this artist, who
is considered a master of innovative technique and style. *Togidashi-e*
(see page 9) was much used in later eighteenth and nineteenth
century prints in an effort to reproduce the colors of *ukiyo-e* prints.
The sheath is decorated with plum branches and a *shimenawa*
[sacred straw rope] suggesting that the dancers are taking part in a
New Year performance.

The Yamamoto Shunshō line of artists worked from the seventeenth
century until the twentieth century and their signatures are seen on
many *inrō* and other lacquer objects.

*Ojime* [bead]: Coral.

### Reference:

Vergez, Robert, *Early Ukiyo-e Master: Okumura Masanobu* (Tokyo and
New York, 1983).

## 45

**MEDICINE-CASE IN FOUR SECTIONS**

11.0 x 6.0 x 3.0 cm.

Signed *Harunobu ga Shōjōsai* [Shōjōsai, after a painting by Harunobu] with a red seal

Twentieth century

This *inrō* is adapted from a woodblock print (publisher unknown, 1767-8) by Suzuki Harunobu (1725-70). A handsomely dressed young dandy is sitting on a veranda, his attention taken by an older woman who is serving as a go-between for her innocent mistress. The shy mistress is seen peeking around a *shōji* [paper screen] on the reverse side of the *inrō*. There is a knowing sexuality in the comportment of the older woman as she transmits her message. This composition is considered one of Harunobu's masterpieces.

Yamaguchi Shōjōsai (1893-1978) was a skilled *inrō* artist who often used *ukiyo-e* woodblock prints as models. In his early years he worked in the Tobe Studio, later becoming independent. Other *inrō* of his with Harunobu designs are known.

*Ojime* [bead]: Cloisonné enamel.

### Reference:

Bushell, Raymond, *The Inrō Handbook* (New York and Tokyo, 1979), 67-8.
Kobayashi, Tadashi, *Ukiyo-e* (Tokyo, New York, and San Francisco, 1982), 9-10.
Wrangham, E. A., *The Index of Inrō Artists* (Harehope, Northumberland, 1995), 249.

46

## MEDICINE-CASE

9.5 x 6.5 x 2.8 cm.
Signed *Somada wo naratte Gyokuzan saku* [made by Gyokuzan, imitating Somada]
Nineteenth century

This sheath *inrō* is in the form of a *gyotai* ['fish purse']. These objects are derived from the *yufu* ['fish-tally'], an emblem of rank made from two closely-fitting parts and worn from the belt by officials in Tang-dynasty (618-907) China. *Gyotai* in Japan were often covered with ray- or fish-skin and inlaid with metal fish as an indication of the owner's wealth and importance. An interior footed tray is decorated with children's toys and emblems of the Gods of Good Fortune (see catalog numbers 47, 63, 72).

The lacquerer Tachibana Gyokuzan worked in Edo in the nineteenth century and often imitated other materials and techniques. For the Somada school, see catalog number 47.

*Ojime* [bead]: Ivory with wire inlay.

### Reference:

Kurokawa, Mayori, 'Hompō fūzoku setsu [On Japanese costume]', *Kokka*, 5 (1895), 180-3.
Laufer, Berthold, *Jade: A Study in Chinese Archaeology and Religion* (New York, 1974; original edn. Chicago, 1912), 220-1.
Wrangham, E. A., *The Index of Inrō Artists* (Harehope, Northumberland, 1995), 63.

47

## MEDICINE-CASE IN FOUR SECTIONS

10.5 x 5.0 x 3.0 cm.
Unsigned
Nineteenth century

Daikoku is one of the Seven Gods of Good Fortune, a group of deities of differing origins representing a blend of popular religious themes. He is the Japanese representation of the Indian deity Mahakala and is recognized as the God of Prosperity, portrayed here packing sacred jewels into a rice bale. Another full bag of treasures is seen on the reverse. The rat is one of Daikoku's attributes and in this context is an emblem of wealth. The top and bottom are decorated with various *takaramono* [precious things], attributes of the Gods of Good Fortune: coins, cloves, the hat and cloak of invisibility, a flaming sacred pearl, merchants' weights, and a scroll.

The *inrō* is in the style of the Somada school of lacquerers (see also catalog number 46), which supposedly originated in the port city of Nagasaki. This is a convincing tradition in view of the fact that their style is a development of Chinese shell-inlay techniques which they could have learned there from Chinese artisans. Somada lacquers use extremely thin iridescent pearl-shell inlays which reflect a palette of shades of green, pink, blue and violet and which are flush with the surface. The thin and colorful shell inlays are referred to by the term *aogai*.

*Ojime* [bead]: Green hardstone.

48

## MEDICINE-CASE IN THREE SECTIONS

11.0 x 6.4 x 2.9 cm.
Unsigned
Nineteenth century

In Daoist mythology Seiōbo (in Chinese, Xiwangmu), is the Queen Mother of the West. She watches over a garden containing the peaches of immortality, which were stolen by Tōbōsaku (Dong-fangshuo). On this *inrō* the goddess is shown on one side and the thief on the reverse. The extensive use of shell inlay alludes to Chinese lacquering techniques and is especially appropriate to this Chinese-derived subject-matter. This type of *inrō* is often referred to as 'Ryūkyū style', but although *inrō* in this style were undoubt-edly produced in the Ryūkyū Islands (present-day Okinawa) it is likely that it was also copied in Japan, perhaps around Nagasaki, the birthplace of the Somada style of shell inlay (see catalog numbers 46-7).

## 49

**MEDICINE-CASE IN FOUR SECTIONS**
8.2 x 5.2 x 2.2 cm.
Signed inside the lid *Koma Kansai*
Nineteenth century

Boats carrying rice are depicted on a fast-flowing river. Mist over the water appears as raised areas of fine gold lacquer which break up the continuous wave pattern. This is an example of the early nineteenth-century revival of the style of Ogata Kōrin (1658-1716), characterized by bold overall designs and dramatic use of lead and shell inlay.

For Koma Kansai, see catalog number 37.

*Ojime* [bead]: Coral.

Netsuke: Wood; inlaid lead boat carrying rice, signed *Taishin* (1825-1903, see catalog number 83).

50

## MEDICINE-CASE IN FOUR SECTIONS
6.8 x 5.5 x 2.1 cm.
Signed *Kanshōsai* with a *kaō* [monogram]
Late eighteenth-nineteenth century

This *inrō* is decorated with a mountainous landscape in the style of an ink-painting. A solitary figure is seen carrying his load of brushwood homeward, dwarfed by the surrounding peaks. The image conveys the humble place of man relative to the grander scheme of nature. The *inrō* artist has remarkably duplicated the feeling of ink on silk or paper by employing black lacquer upon a silver mound. This technique is called *togidashi sumi-e* (see also catalog number 69 and page 9).

Kanshōsai is one of the art-names of Iizuka Tōyō or Tōyōsai, who was active in the second half of the eighteenth century. The same design, also executed in *togidashi sumi-e*, is seen on *inrō* signed *Koma Kansai* and *Koma Kyūhaku*.

*Ojime* [bead]: Black lacquer.

### Reference:
Von Ragué, Beatrix, 'Materialien zu Iizuka Tōyō, seinem Werk und seiner Schule', *Oriens Extremus*, 11/2 (December 1964), 163-235.

## 51

### MEDICINE-CASE IN FOUR SECTIONS

8.8 x 6.7 x 1.7 cm.
Signed *Koma Yasutada saku* [made by Koma Yasutada]
Nineteenth century

Over a period of almost fourteen centuries, pilgrims and sightseers have flocked to Mount Yoshino in Yamato Province to view the flowering of the cherry-blossoms in April of each year. The trees, 'which are supposed to number exactly a thousand, but are really much more numerous', were first planted by a Buddhist priest in the seventh century. The beautiful scenery has been the subject of many poems, paintings and works of applied art. The lacquerer has depicted the cherry flowers by inlaying with silver each individual petal of every flower. The hills are highlighted by *okibirame* [small, individually placed, square inlays of gold], and as one moves into the distance and to the top of the *inrō* the hills and trees enter a mist. All these latter motifs are rendered in *togidashi-e* (see page 9).

The name Yasutada was first used by Koma Kyūhaku (*d.* 1715) but few lacquers with this signature are thought to date from earlier than the third quarter of the eighteenth century.

*Ojime* [bead]: Hardstone.

**Reference:**

Chamberlain, Basil H., *A Handbook for Travellers in Japan* (London, 1901), 372.

Wrangham, E. A., *The Index of Inrō Artists* (Harehope, Northumberland, 1995), 327-8.

## 52

**MEDICINE-CASE IN FOUR SECTIONS**
9.4 x 5.4 x 2.2 cm.
Unsigned
Nineteenth century

A bamboo grove in mist depicted in various shades of *togidashi-e*.
This atmospheric design is also seen on an *inrō* in the Baur
Collection which bears the seal of Shiomi Masanari, a specialist in
this technique (see catalog nos. 53-5).

**Reference:**
Schneeberger, Pierre-F., *Japanese Lacquer (Selected Pieces)* [in the Baur
   Collection, Geneva] (Geneva, 1984), cat. no. F.90.

53

## MEDICINE-CASE IN FOUR SECTIONS
7.5 x 6.0 x 2.5 cm.
Signed in seal form *Shiomi Masanari*
Nineteenth century

Depicted on this sheath *inrō* are night fishermen, who exploit the light provided by the flames of firepots hanging from their boats in order to attract their prey. In this case, each boat is fitted with nets which are supported by bamboo struts and then immersed in the sea. The nets are raised and the catch placed in baskets which are centrally placed in the boat.

Shiomi Masanari lived from 1647 to 1722 and his characteristic seal-style signature was used by a large number of artists during the following two centuries.

**Reference:**
Wrangham, E. A., *The Index of Inrō Artists* (Harehope, Northumberland, 1995), 167.

## 54

**MEDICINE-CASE IN FOUR SECTIONS**
7.5 x 5.0 x 2.0 cm.
Signed in seal form *Shiomi Masanari*
Late eighteenth-nineteenth century

The subject of the ox and herdsman is among the classic parables used to explain the spiritual basis of Zen. These parables were used to promote an understanding of man's own nature. The parable begins with the herdsman falling asleep and the ox wandering off. The way of Zen is then explained in a set of ten 'parable pictures' depicting the ox being sought, found, caught, and ultimately returned home.

This subject, depicted in *togidashi-e* (see page 9), was a favorite of Shiomi Masanari's (see catalog number 53).

*Ojime* [bead]: Coral.

**Reference:**

Brinker, Helmut, *Zen in the Art of Painting* (London and New York, 1987), 103-9.
Fontein, Jan, and Hickman, Money L., *Zen Painting and Calligraphy* (exhibition catalog, November 5-December 20, 1970; Boston and Greenwich, Connecticut, 1970), 113-8.

55

## MEDICINE-CASE IN ONE SECTION

7.2 x 8.5 x 3.5 cm.
Signed in seal form *Shiomi Masanari*
Nineteenth century

This *inrō* decorated with dragonflies is modeled to imitate a leather tobacco pouch. The dragonfly is emblematic of Japan and is a popular motif in Japanese art. The green lacquer ground, with finely sprinkled gold, is meant to represent embossed leather as would be appropriate for a tobacco-pouch. The silver clasp is modeled as a demon-mask.

For Shiomi Masanari, see catalog number 53.

*Ojime* [bead]: Soft metal.

56

## MEDICINE-CASE IN FOUR SECTIONS
7.3 x 5.5 x 2.5 cm.
Unsigned
Nineteenth century

A solitary black cicada sits on each side of the *inrō*, having alighted upon a bamboo fence. This insect is highly thought of in East Asia. The Chinese first noted the complex life cycle of the cicada, which places its eggs under the bark of a tree limb from where the larva migrate to the roots and slowly develop over a period of years, whence they emerge from the ground as an adult insect. The cicada thus exemplifies the Buddhist doctrine of perpetual rebirth and eternal life.

*Ojime* [bead]: Quartz crystal.

Netsuke: Hornbill; a minutely detailed cicada.

**Reference:**
Schneeberger, Pierre-F., *Japanese Lacquer (Selected Pieces)* [The Baur Collection, Geneva] (Geneva, 1984), cat. no. F161.

## 57

## MEDICINE-CASE IN ONE SECTION
6.4 x 8.6 x 3.3 cm.
Unsigned
Nineteenth century

This *inrō* simulates the form of a leather tobacco-pouch, the metal clasp being represented by a spider. The design of insects caught in a spider's web was popular in the nineteenth century, being seen, for example in the ink-painting of Ukita Ikkei (1795-1859) and the lacquers of Shibata Zeshin (1807-91, see catalog numbers 67-82), whose work may have inspired the present example.

**Reference:**

Earle, Joe and Gōke, Tadaomi, *Meiji no Takara, Treasures of Imperial Japan, Masterpieces by Shibata Zeshin* (London, 1996), cat. nos. 17, 83.

Watson, William (ed.), *The Great Japan Exhibition: Art of the Edo Period* (Exhibition catalogue, London, Royal Academy of Arts, October 24, 1981-February 21, 1982; London, 1981), cat. no. 88.

58

## MEDICINE-CASE IN FOUR SECTIONS

9.0 x 6.0 x 1.7 cm.
Signed *Koma Yasutada saku* [made by Koma Yasutada]
Late eighteenth century-nineteenth century

In both China and Japan the peony is held in the highest esteem
and is considered 'King of Flowers'. Among the attributes accorded
the peony are good fortune, power and wealth. It also symbolizes
the paradise of the bodhisattva Monju, from a No play by Zeami
(1363-1443) in which a lion, Monju's mount, appears and dances
in a field of peonies. Both the herbaceous peony (*shakuyaku*) and
the tree peony (*botan*) are common themes in East Asian art.

For Koma Yasutada, see catalog number 51.

*Ojime* [bead]: *Shakudō* (see catalog number 64); flowers.

### Reference:

Meech, Julia, *Lacquerware from the Weston Collection, A Selection of Inro
    and Boxes* (New York, 1995), cat. no. 13.
Smithers, Peter, 'Moutan', *Arts of Asia*, 14/2 (March-April 1984), 55-61.

136

59

## MEDICINE-CASE IN FOUR SECTIONS
9.1 x 6.8 x 1.9 cm.
Signed *Nariyuki saku* [made by Nariyuki] with a seal *Imaizumi*
Early twentieth century

Cock-fighting is documented as having been practised in Japan as early as the fifteenth century but the fighting cock appears more frequently in eighteenth-century and later art. Its popularity in Japan may have reflected their re-introduction by the Dutch. These beautiful and belligerent creatures appear similar to those seen in the Dutch East Indies (Indonesia), in particular the trading post of Bantan in Java, from which the name 'Bantam rooster' is derived. A group of spectators is depicted on the reverse, together with two bamboo bird-cages.

Several examples of this design by Imaizumi Nariyuki (also called Seishi) are known. He is thought to have worked around the second and third decades of the present century.

*Ojime* [bead]: Hardstone.

### Reference:
Meech, Julia, *Lacquerware from the Weston Collection, A Selection of Inro and Boxes* (New York, 1995), cat. no. 94.
Takao Yō, 'Kinsei makie-shi meikan 4 [A list of Edo- and Meiji-period *maki-e* artists, part 4]', *Rokushō*, 20 (1996), (104-10), 104.
Wrangham, E. A., *The Index of Inrō Artists* (Harehope, Northumberland, 1995), 199.

## 60

### MEDICINE-CASE IN FOUR SECTIONS
8.5 x 5.7 x 2.0 cm.
Signed *Inagawa*, with a vase-shaped seal *Nakaharu*
Nineteenth century

The diminutive *shika* [dappled deer] of Japan are depicted under a maple tree, in a scene that has symbolized the autumn season for more than a thousand years.

The Inagawa school, probably an offshoot of the Kajikawa line (see catalog number 41), copied the Kajikawa practice of concluding their signatures with a vase-shaped seal.

*Ojime* [bead]: Coral.

Netsuke: Ivory; a reclining deer licking her flank, unsigned (Osaka; Garaku school, eighteenth century).

61

## MEDICINE-CASE IN FOUR SECTIONS

9.5 x 5.9 x 1.2 cm.
Ivory
Unsigned
Nineteenth century

The decoration of this dramatic *inrō* consists of a large *ebi* [crayfish or lobster] carved from many layers of lacquer in the *tsuishu* technique (see page 9). The *ebi*'s crooked back, symbolizing longevity, and auspicious red color make it a favorite motif at the New Year celebrations, where it was used to decorate gateways. The decoration is probably by a member of the Yōsei dynasty of craftsmen, which lasted from the fourteenth to the twentieth century.

**Reference:**

Chamberlain, Basil H., *Things Japanese* (fourth edition; London, 1902), 158.

62

## MEDICINE-CASE IN FOUR SECTIONS
8.3 x 5.7 x 2.4 cm.
Signed *Oyama saku* [made by Oyama]
Late nineteenth or twentieth century

The whaling industry of nineteenth century Japan used heroic centuries-old methods which contrasted greatly with those employed in the West. Whaling was practised in the southernmost areas of the islands of Honshu and Shikoku; one Shikoku whaler, Nakahama (John) Manjirō (1827-98), was blown off course and finished up in Honolulu in autumn 1841. Spotters were placed as lookouts at the highest points on the cliffs. At the earliest dawn, when the sun turned the sky a golden vermilion, the plumes exhaled by the whales would become illuminated. This view from the cliffs would be reported to the fleet by signal flags and the little boats would embark on a chase to net and capture the whale. The black right whale is depicted among silvery waves beneath a golden-red sunrise. A magnificent wave breaks across the tail of this grand animal and eddies swirl about its body.

The attempt to depict the fragile grace and yet the power and violence of the wave has been a goal of many Japanese artists. It could be argued that the wave accomplished by Oyama on this *inrō* joins this illustrious company.

Nothing is known of Oyama (see also catalog number 2). His signature is seen on only a small number of *inrō* and he is considered by some authorities to be a twentieth- rather than a late nineteenth-century artist.

*Ojime* [bead]: *Umimatsu* [petrified coral].

Netsuke: Ivory; a sperm whale.

**Reference:**
Bernard, Donald R., *The Life and Times of John Manjiro* (New York, 1992), 6-26.
Nicol, Clive W., *Harpoon: A Novel* (New York, 1987).

63

**SAKE-CUP**
Dia. 18.7 cm.
Unsigned
Nineteenth century

Within the hollow of the cup is a mallet, the attribute of Daikoku, one of the Gods of Good Fortune. Daikoku is the God of Prosperity and is usually portrayed sitting among sacks filled with rice and riches. On the reverse side of the cup is a hat which represents the Household God Ebisu. Also present is Ebisu's familiar, the *tai* [sea bream], and a bamboo fishing pole. Ebisu frequently accompanies Daikoku and his presence represents the availability of plentiful amounts of food. The auspicious theme makes it likely that this ceremonial cup was made for use at a wedding ceremony.

64

## MEDICINE-CASE IN FOUR SECTIONS
9.0 x 4.5 x 2.6 cm.
Signed for the metalwork on two engraved gold plaques *Mon Eijō*
[design by Eijō] and *Mitsuteru*, with a *kaō* [monogram]
Mid-nineteenth century

Sea-shells were a favored subject of several eighteenth-century artists. Perhaps the most famous of these was Kitagawa Utamaro (1754-1806). Seven sea shells of gold and other alloys including *shakudō*, a patinated mixture of copper with a tiny percentage of gold, are inlaid onto a continuous pattern of waves subtly drawn in *yamimaki-e* [black low relief against a black lacquer ground]. The signatures refer to two masters of the Gotō school whose members combined the roles of official mint-masters and manufacturers of the most formal sword-fittings, using a particularly attractive violaceous *shakudō*. Mitsuteru, also called Mitsutoshi (1816-56), is considered to have restored the family's reputation for high-quality work in formal style and was rewarded for his services to the shogunate with a substantial stipend. Nineteenth-century *inrō* with inlaid metalwork often also incorporate a design attribution to a much earlier Gotō master, in this case Eijō, also called Masamitsu (1577-1617), the sixth head of the school.

*Ojime* [bead]: Pearl.

Netsuke: Black lacquer; sea shells, signed *Tomonobu*.

**Reference:**
Wakayama, Hōmatsu (Takeshi), *Kinkō jiten* [A dictionary of sword-fitting makers] (Tokyo, 1972), 45-6 and 432.

65

**STORAGE-BOX**
28.0 x 34.0 x 22.5 cm.
Unsigned
Nineteenth century

This storage box is made of rare *keyaki* [zelkova] wood, with bold and elegant silver mounts embellished with chrysanthemums. The inside of the front lid of this box is decorated in dramatic contrast with a gold lacquer design showing three puppies and the three emblems of winter (pine, bamboo, and plum) in the manner of the Shijō school (see also catalog number 82). Through the influence of such painters as Matsumura Goshun (1752-1811) and his pupil Keibun (1779-1843), these informal animal motifs are often seen on later Edo-period lacquer.

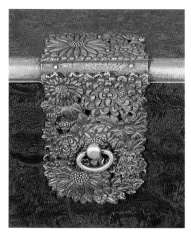

Detail of metalwork clasp

66

## PIPE-CASE

21 x 3.2 x 1.7 cm.
Unsigned
Nineteenth century

The birds and foliage represented on this pipe-case are an example
of the *chōshitsu* [carved lacquer] technique. In this example the
image was created by the application of numerous thin layers of
lacquer of alternating color, yellow, red, green, and black, ending
with a final layer of black. The artist then carved into the lacquer
at different depths, using the different colors he revealed in this
way to obtain a three-dimensional multi-colored image (see page
9).

Detail

67

## BOX
8.0 x 17.0 x 24.0 cm.
Signed *Shibata Zeshin*
*Circa* 1860-90

Zeshin has depicted the waves, seaweed and shells along a shoreline in the most subtle of ways. The waves are combed in the *seigaiha* technique (see also catalog number 7) and barely contrast with the background coloration of the box. The seashells scratched into the lacquer are said to have been done using a sharpened rat's tooth. The seaweed has a highly textured surface and is colored green, but nevertheless blends with the background. Shibata Zeshin's (1807-91) restrained designs, using a range of subdued techniques developed during the 1840s, call to mind the 'artless', self-effacing aesthetic of the tea ceremony which is often referred to outside Japan by the adjective *shibui* [astringent]. In Japan, however, Zeshin is rather seen as embodying the spirit of *iki*, defined by Gōke Tadaomi as 'light and unconstrained, gallant without being obstinate, playful but never tiresome, assertive but not argumentative...'.

**Reference:**

Gōke, Tadaomi, *Shibata Zeshin eyō tebikae* [Sketches and notes by Shibata Zeshin] (Tokyo, 1981), 5.

## 68

## MEDICINE-CASE IN FOUR SECTIONS
7.8 x 5.6 x 2.4 cm.
Signed *Zeshin*
1890

Supernatural phenomena were popular subjects in nineteenth-century Japan. In Japanese Buddhist folklore, spirits are believed to reside in a world suspended between the living and the dead. When a person dies in a state of emotional unrest, the spirit may return to the world of the living as a ghost.

This *inrō* by Shibata Zeshin (1807-91) shows a female ghost peering over a green mosquito net; the same design is seen in a woodblock print designed by Ochiai Yoshiiku (1833-1904) in 1890, the year before Zeshin's death which, very unusually, bears Zeshin's seal as well as the artist's signature. The image probably derives from the work of the painter Kawanabe Kyōsai (1831-89) who specialized in the depiction of ghosts, a subject generally avoided by Zeshin. Here he takes the technique of lacquerwork to its very limits, ignoring the limited palette and unforgiving nature of the medium and exploiting the advantages of the metallic silver powders to produce a ghostly complexion which cannot be readily duplicated by other techniques. One of the characteristics of Zeshin is the tendency to scratch an element into the lacquer composition. Here he has scratched a mosquito, which rests on the lamp.

*Ojime* [bead]: Ivory; a skull rendered in accurate anatomic detail.

Netsuke: Ivory; a female ghost with no lower limbs, signed *Masatoshi*.

**Reference:**

Clark, Timothy, *Demon of Painting: The Art of Kawanabe Kyōsai* (exhibition catalog, British Museum, December 1, 1993-February 13, 1994; London, 1993), cat. nos. 29-32.

Jordan, Brenda, '*Yurei*: Tales of Female Ghosts' and Yamamoto, A.Y., 'Japanese Ghosts and Demons: Art of the Supernatural', in Addiss, Stephen (ed.), *Japanese Ghosts and Demons: Art of the Supernatural* (exhibition catalog, June 13-September 1, 1985; New York and Lawrence, Kansas, 1985), 25-33

Woodblock print signed *Yoshiiku* with seal *Zeshin*, 1890. 25 cm x 18.1 cm

A mosquito has alighted upon the andon [lamp]. The insect was scratched into the lacquer by Zeshin.

69

## MEDICINE-CASE IN TWO SECTIONS

7.5 x 8.4 x 3.3 cm.
Signed *Zeshin* with a red seal *Koma*
*Circa* 1860-90

The story of the *Shitakiri-suzume* [Tongue-Cut Sparrow], shown on this *inrō*, tells of a kind-hearted farmer and his ill-tempered wife who had a pet sparrow. One day the woman punished the sparrow for eating her laundry starch by cutting its tongue, and the wounded bird flew to its home in the forest. When the husband arrived home he heard about the punishment and entered the forest to help the sparrow. As he was a good man, the bird offered him hospitality and the choice of either a large or a small basket as a gift. The man chose the small basket and returned home. When he opened it he found silk, gold and jewels. This encouraged the mean old woman to embark upon the same journey. She was also offered her choice of baskets. She greedily chose the larger basket, expecting even greater riches. However, when she opened this basket, monsters, ghosts and goblins, jumped out and avenged the tongue-cut sparrow.

When the *inrō* is closed the basket already seems to be half open, with goblins beginning to emerge. When the sections are separated, the risers can be seen to be decorated with more monsters in *togidashi sumi-e* technique (see catalog number 50), a touch typical of the artistry of Shibata Zeshin (1807-91). The seal *Koma*, seen on this piece, is a reference to Zeshin's schooling in the workshop of Koma Kansai II (see catalog number 37).

*Ojime* [bead]: Lacquer; plum-blossoms.

Netsuke: Lacquer; a sparrow, signed *Taishin* (1825-1903) with a *kaō* [monogram].

**Reference:**
Mayer, Fanny H., *Ancient Tales in Modern Japan* (Bloomington, Indiana, 1984), no. 126 (p.143).

70

## MEDICINE-CASE IN THREE SECTIONS

7.0 x 5.4 x 2.8 cm.
Signed *Zeshin*
*Circa* 1860-90

The subject of this *inrō* by Shibata Zeshin (1807-91) is the battle of
Dan no Ura (1185). During the twelfth century two powerful clans,
the Taira and the Minamoto, struggled for supremacy and sought
to legitimate their power by controlling the person of the Emperor.
The Taira clan had the child Emperor Antoku (1178-85; reigned
1181-3) hidden away in the temple at Itsukushima. The head priest
gave Antoku's guardian Nii no Ama, widow of the Taira leader
Kiyomori, a fan with the design of a red disk which was said to
have magical protective properties. The fan was fixed to the mast
of a Taira ship holding the Emperor in a fleet which challenged the
Minamoto naval forces at Dan no Ura. A Minamoto warrior, Nasu
no Yoichi, rode his horse into the surf and launched an arrow which
struck and shattered the retaining-pin of the fan. With the loss of
this talisman the Taira were defeated and Nii no Ama threw herself
into the sea with the seven-year-old Antoku.

On this *inrō* the Taira boat lies adrift behind a pine tree with a bare
mast; the butterfly insignia of the clan can be seen on two boards.
On the reverse, the shattered fan flies through the air, as does the
arrow shot by Nasu no Yoichi.

*Ojime* [bead]: Metal.

Netsuke: Lacquer, *manjū* [flat circular] type; boats carrying fire-
wood, signed *Koma Bunsai* (nineteenth century).

**Reference:**
Joly, Henri L., *Legend in Japanese Art* (London, 1908), 366.

## 71

## MEDICINE-CASE IN THREE SECTIONS

7.6 x 5.0 x 1.5 cm.
Signed *Zeshin*
*Circa* 1860-90

On this *inrō* a fox has disguised itself as a priest. The Japanese fox exhibits a variety of supernatural traits, including the ability to disguise itself in various human forms. The fox is a clever trickster, frequently a female, who gets a great deal of satisfaction from seducing, frightening or otherwise tormenting man. This *inrō* is a lighthearted parody and a commentary on corruption, deviousness and hypocrisy which some perceived to exist among certain members of the Buddhist priesthood. Shibata Zeshin (1807-91) did an ink-painting on the same subject. The reverse of the *inrō* shows a *naruko* [bird-scarer] and grasses.

*Ojime* [bead]: Green hardstone.

Netsuke: Lacquered wood; rabbits preparing rice-cakes, signed *Zeshin*.

### Reference:

Earle, Joe and Gōke, Tadaomi, *Meiji no Takara, Treasures of Imperial Japan, Masterpieces by Shibata Zeshin* (London, 1996), cat. no. 96.

Jordan, Brenda, 'The Trickster in Japan: *Tanuki* and *Kitsune*', in Addiss, Stephen (ed.), *Japanese Ghosts and Demons: Art of the Supernatural* (exhibition catalog, June 13-September 1, 1985; New York and Lawrence, Kansas, 1985), 25-33.

Link, Howard A., *The Art of Shibata Zeshin* (Honolulu, 1979), cat. no. 68.

Painting of a fox priest by Shibata Zeshin. Hanging scroll, ink on paper. 43.5 x 117 cm. Courtesy Robyn Buntin.

72

## MEDICINE-CASE IN FOUR SECTIONS

9.0 x 6.9 x 2.0 cm.
Signed *Zeshin*
*Circa* 1860-90

The rat is the first animal of the East Asian zodiac and occupies a position of respect, in dramatic contrast to Western attitudes about rodents. In Japan the rat is a symbol of prosperity and industriousness, particularly associated with the popular deity Daikoku. While there is practical realism to Western views of rats as vermin, the more benign Asian view allows the rat to be pleasantly represented in Japanese art. The Gods of Good Fortune and their attributes are often seen in the work of Shibata Zeshin (1807-91), who never lost his affection for the popular culture of the Edo townsfolk.

A black lacquer rat crawls across the top of the *inrō*, where a partly eaten red lacquer *tōgarashi* [pepper] has discharged its seed. Footprints are incised into the lacquer by using a sharp implement such as a rat's tooth.

The *tōgarashi* is frequently represented in Zeshin's lacquer and is thought to be a reference to the proverb *keshi ga karakerya tōgarashi ga inkyo suru* [if the mustard-seed is too strong, the taste of the chilli is smothered], alluding to the adjective *keshikaranu*, meaning 'uncouth' or 'uncool', in other words the direct opposite of everything that Zeshin sought to achieve in lacquer.

*Ojime* [bead]: Coral.

Netsuke: Wood; a rat eating through the lid of a large rice bowl.

### Reference:

Gōke, Tadaomi, 'The Lacquerware of Shibata Zeshin - An Appreciation', in Earle, Joe and Gōke, Tadaomi, *Meiji no Takara, Treasures of Imperial Japan, Masterpieces by Shibata Zeshin* (London, 1996), 18-20.

73

## MEDICINE-CASE IN ONE SECTION
5.0 x 5.8 x 2.0 cm.
Signed *Zeshin*
*Circa* 1860-90

This *inrō* is in the form of a chest which a samurai warrior would use to store his armor. The class structure of the Edo period (1615-1868) placed samurai in the highest social category and craftsmen like Shibata Zeshin (1807-91) in the lowest. In Zeshin's art there is often a sense of nostalgia for the past coupled with relief at the passing of the feudal restrictions of the Edo period (1615-1868). This contradiction is expressed here by the image of the powerless empty armor-sleeve draped over the box.

74

## BOX

2.7 x 7.4 x 9.3 cm.
Signed *Zeshin*
*Circa* 1879-90

This box appears to be made of rosewood: the grain and color are true to the actual material and at one corner of the cover there appears a crack which has undergone repair using a butterfly shaped-cleat and a metal staple. In fact, the box is made of papier mâché and the entire design is of lacquer in the *shitan-nuri* technique, the most elaborate of the many new surfaces developed by Shibata Zeshin (1807-91) during the 1840s and 1850s. The wood grain has been carefully scratched into the surface of the lacquer. The crack is simulated, also having been scratched, probably with a sharp rat's tooth.

Zeshin used a very similar design, including the same butterfly-shaped cleat, in an album of lacquer paintings which he produced between about 1879 and 1890.

**Published:**

Lazarnick, George, *Netsuke and Inrō Artists and How to Read Their Signatures* (Honolulu, 1982), 1271.

**Reference:**

Earle, Joe and Gōke, Tadaomi, *Meiji no Takara, Treasures of Imperial Japan, Masterpieces by Shibata Zeshin* (London, 1996), cat. no. 76.13.

75

## BOX

10.3 x 7.5 x 4.2 cm.
Signed *Zeshin*
*Circa* 1860-90

This box of lacquered leather simulates a physician's receptacle for storing leeches. The artist has created an unusual lacquer surface which has a crude metallic character. The wooden lid of the container is carved in order to give the impression of rotting wood. Two leeches cling to the outside. The employment of a sophisticated lacquer technique for such a simple subject reflects the virtuosity of this artist.

### Reference:

Earle, Joe and Gōke, Tadaomi, *Meiji no Takara, Treasures of Imperial Japan, Masterpieces by Shibata Zeshin* (London, 1996), cat. nos. 15, 65, where the leeches are identified as nails.

76

## NETSUKE

Dia. 4.0 cm.
Signed *Zeshin*
*Circa* 1860-90

This sparrow-shaped miniature sculpture is an abstraction, capturing the bird's graceful, rounded image with extreme economy. The surface is lacquered in a textured brown-green color called *seidō-nuri* [bronze lacquer] which was developed by Shibata Zeshin (1807-91) in the 1840s. A chrysanthemum pattern and a *tomoe-mon* [comma-pattern crest] appear on the sparrow's back.

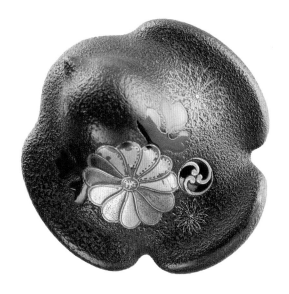

## 77

## SET OF MOUNTS FOR A DAGGER
41.0 x 3.9 1.8 cm.
Signed *Zeshin*
*Circa* 1860-90

During the Edo period (1615-1868) only samurai were, in theory, allowed to own and wear edged weapons. The large number of extant daggers and *wakizashi* [short swords] in a nineteenth-century style and with distinctly un-samurai-like decoration would suggest, however, that this law was ignored during the closing years of the period, leading up to the abolition of sword-wearing in 1876. Zeshin made several sets of sword-mounts both on his own and in collaboration with other artists such as the great metalworker Kano Natsuo (1828-98). This example is decorated on a rough wood ground with paulownia-crests and other motifs in a variety of techniques, taking full advantage of the contrast between the deeply pitted surface and the carefully finished lacquer.

### Reference:
Earle, Joe and Gōke, Tadaomi, *Meiji no Takara, Treasures of Imperial Japan, Masterpieces by Shibata Zeshin* (London, 1996), cat. no. 49.

Detail

Detail

## 78

## PIPE-CASE
21.0 x 2.8 cm.
Signed *Zeshin*
*Circa* 1860-90

This *kiseruzutsu* [pipe-case] is an outstanding example of the application of the most refined aesthetic to the decoration of simple objects. Shibata Zeshin's (1807-91) asymmetric composition of a dying dandelion is an example of the heights reached by the finest lacquer artists when they decorated such everyday objects.

*Ojime* [bead]: Jadeite.

Tobacco-pouch: fine cotton with a *shibuichi* [copper and silver alloy] butterfly clasp.

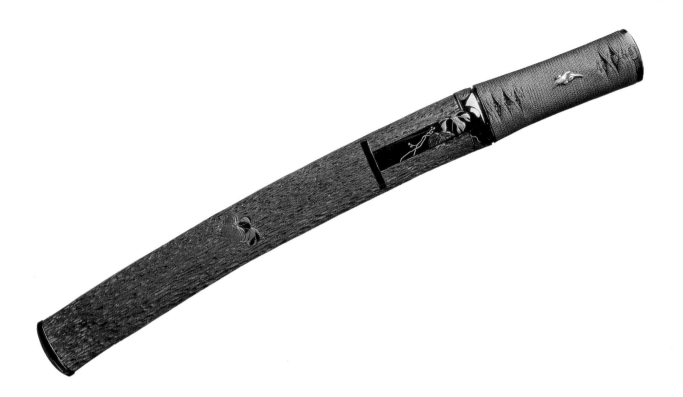

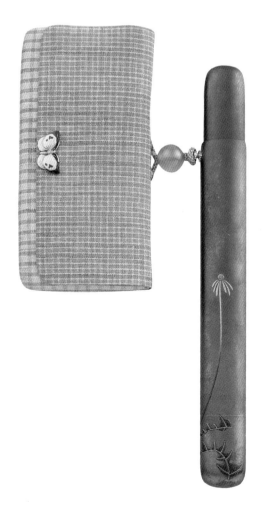

79

## LACQUER PAINTING

33 x 46 cm.
Signed *Zeshin* with a seal *Koma*
*Circa* 1872-90

This scroll of a grasshopper on a flowering gourd, depicted in minute detail, is an example of the innovative genius of Shibata Zeshin (1807-91), who in 1872 adapted the medium of lacquer for the purpose of painting directly onto a prepared paper surface. Given the unforgivingly viscous nature of this medium and its hardening characteristics, the development of this technique must be considered a resounding achievement. The song of the grasshopper is an appreciated sign of autumn in Japan, as is the appearance of the gourd vines depicted here.

Zeshin often appended the family name of his lacquer-master, Koma Kansai (see catalog number 37), to his works in this medium.

**Reference:**

Earle, Joe, 'Shibata Zeshin: Technique, Style and Dating', in Earle, Joe and Gōke, Tadaomi, *Meiji no Takara, Treasures of Imperial Japan, Masterpieces by Shibata Zeshin* (London, 1996), 28-30.
Earle, Joe and Gōke, Tadaomi, *Meiji no Takara, Treasures of Imperial Japan, Masterpieces by Shibata Zeshin* (London, 1996), cat. nos. 82.1, 83.

80

## LACQUER PAINTING

15.6 x 19.2 cm.
Signed *Zeshin* with a seal *Koma*
*Circa* 1872-90

The painting shows a collection of pottery and porcelain objects which might decorate a tea-house. A Tamba stoneware jar contains branches of budding plum blossoms. A red camellia is seen beside an Imari porcelain teapot with polychrome enamel decoration. The use of lacquer as a medium allows the Tamba jar to take on the rough, heavy, folk art appearance which makes these stoneware jars a favorite of tea-ceremony devotees. The teapot is accomplished in a range of colored lacquers including the use of rare white lacquer to give the appearance of natural porcelain. The background is black lacquer on a gold leaf base. Shibata Zeshin (1807-91) loved to imitate other materials in this demanding medium.

81

## FAN-SHAPED LACQUER PAINTING
50.0 x 17.5 cm.
With a seal *Zeshin*
*Circa* 1872-90

This characteristically bold composition is dominated by a huge *ebi* [crayfish or lobster] whose long whiskers follow the curve of the fan over to the right-hand side. Perhaps because of its association with longevity, during the last few years of his life Zeshin often depicted the *ebi* in painting and lacquer, sometimes as here dominating the composition, sometimes tossed against its will by enormous waves. Of three large *ebi* panels dating from 1888 and 1889, one received a gold medal in Paris in 1889, one was shown at the Third National Industrial Exposition in Tokyo in 1890, and a probable third is in the Khalili collection.

### Reference:
Earle, Joe and Gōke, Tadaomi, *Meiji no Takara, Treasures of Imperial Japan, Masterpieces by Shibata Zeshin* (London, 1996), cat. no. 28.
Gōke Tadaomi, 'Shitsugei no sui: Zeshin sakuhin [The essence of lacquer art: works by Zeshin]', *Me no me*, 241 (October 1996), (21-8), 27

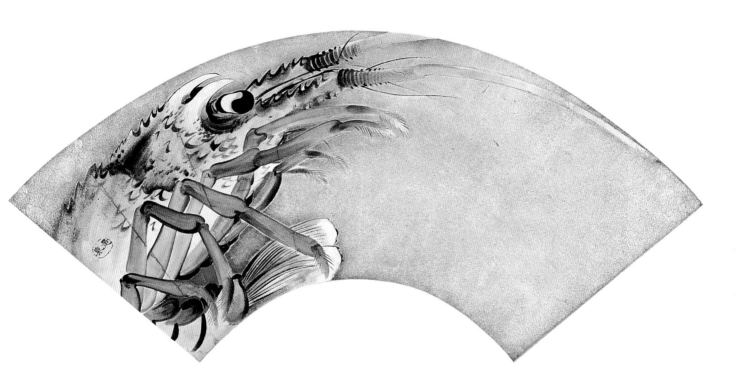

82

**FAN-SHAPED LACQUER PAINTING**
48.0 x 14.0 cm.
Signed *Zeshin*, with a seal
*Circa* 1872-90

Two puppies are subtly represented with a few simple strokes of
lacquer in the manner of the Shijō school. During his apprectice
years, Zeshin not only mastered the techniques of lacquering under
Koma Kansai II; he also studied painting with two leading masters
associated with the Shijō school, Suzuki Nanrei (1775-1844) in Edo
and Okamoto Toyohiko (1773-1845) in Kyoto. The influence of
these two artists is felt in much of his work on paper, whether in
ink or in his special medium of lacquer painting.

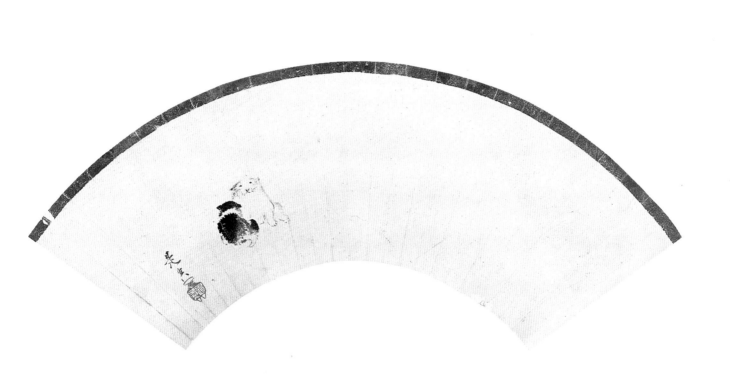

83

## WRITING-BOX
3.0 x 12.5 x 21.0 cm.
Signed *Taishin*
*Circa* 1860-90

A *daikon* [radish] surrounded by a variety of vegetables is represented on a stylized *mokume* ground imitating wood-grain. The
base is decorated with a basket-weave pattern over further vegetable designs.

Ikeda Taishin (1825-1903) was Zeshin's most prominent pupil and
considered an outstanding lacquer artist in his own right. In 1896
he was created a member of the Imperial Household Artist
(*Teishitsu gigeiin*) order, like his master Zeshin, who received this
honor in 1890.

### Reference:
Gōke, Tadaomi, 'The Lacquerware of Shibata Zeshin - An Appreciation',
in Earle, Joe and Gōke, Tadaomi, *Meiji no Takara, Treasures of Imperial
Japan, Masterpieces by Shibata Zeshin* (London, 1996), 22.

84

## MEDICINE-CASE IN FOUR SECTIONS
8.6 x 5.0 x 2.0 cm.
Signed *Jikan Gambun*
Nineteenth century

Insects arc frequently depicted in Japanese art. The Chinese character for ant (*gi, ari*), if separated into its two constituent parts, can be translated as 'righteous insect' and ants are admired in Japan for their industry, highly organized social structure, and powers of recovery from adversity. A well known postwar haiku poem by Saitō Mitsuki, dating from 1948, sums up the Japanese fascination with their ceaseless activity:

*Haka no mae*
*tsuyoki ari ite*
*honsō su*

In front of the grave
powerful ants are running
hither and thither

'Gamboun est le chantre de la gent fourmilière' [Gambun sings the praises of the ant race] wrote Louis Gonse in his book *L'art Japonais*, published in 1886. This eloquently expresses the manner in which this artist dedicated his work to the natural world of which rot and recycling are a part and which is inhabited by the ant and the snail, his favorite creatures.

*Ojime* [bead]: Soft metal; a snail.

Netsuke: Wood; ants on a pile of chestnuts.

### Reference:
Gonse, Louis, *L'art Japonais* (Paris, 1886), 192.
Matsumoto Seichō, *Tsuyoki ari* [The powerful ant] (Tokyo, 1974), 367.

85

## PIPE-CASE

22.0 x 2.6 cm.
Signed *Hashiichi*
Nineteenth century

This pipe-case is of carved wood which has been expertly shaped
and lacquered to simulate bamboo. The artist is so accomplished
in this technique that only close inspection reveals the true nature
of the object. Hashiichi (Hashimoto Ichizō, 1817-82) specialized in
the production of pieces which appeared to be made from bamboo
and other natural materials.

### Reference:

Ducros, Alain, *Netsuke & Sagemono 2* (Granges-les-Valence, 1987), 189.
Jirka-Schmitz, Patrizia, 'Trompe-l'oeil, simulation and imitation in the
    decorative arts of the Meiji period', *Andon*, 7/27-8 (1987), 73-85, fig. 6.

86

## PIPE-CASE
20.5 x 3.2 x 1.5 cm.
Signed in seal form *Rosetsu*
Late nineteenth century or early twentieth century

The relief decoration on this pipe-case accentuates the powerful, tall, and graceful crests of the waves interspersed with swirling eddies. The artist employs dark blue lacquer, intricately carved to emphasize the violence of the sea.

The seal *Rosetsu*, used by Maeyama Kōshin, appears on several pieces of carved lacquer of the Meiji period (1868-1912) and perhaps also of the Taisho period (1912-26).

### Reference:
Gōke, Tadaomi, Hutt, Julia, and Wrangham, E. A., *Meiji no Takara, Treasures of Imperial Japan, Lacquer* (London, 1995), cat. no. 108, misread *Ransetsu*.
Wrangham, E. A., *The Index of Inrō Artists* (Harehope, Northumberland, 1995), 150.

87

## WRITING-BOX

3.3 x 16.0 x 22.8 cm.
Inscribed on the storage box *Asayama*
Late nineteenth or early twentieth century

A stag-beetle is seen climbing upon a fallen leaf. The mirror-black
beetle is set off from the equally black background by a rotting leaf
which is of silver alloy with golden highlights. The characteristic
appreciation of nature by the Japanese artist allows this lowly beetle
and the rotting leaf to be depicted as beautiful components of the
natural world. The asymmetry of the composition is a characteristically Japanese artistic device, as is the undecorated background.

## 88

## PIPE-CASE

24.0 x 3.0 x 1.4 cm.

Signed *Shōsai* with a seal *Shōsai*; the storage box also signed *Shōsai*, with a *kaō* [monogram]
Late nineteenth-early twentieth century

The subject of this pipe-case is the *nadeshiko* [Dianthus superbus, see also catalog number 6], a flower celebrated since the eighth century as one of the *nanakusa* [seven autumn grasses]; the word *nadeshiko* is also often taken to refer to a small child. In Chapter Two, *Hahakigi* [The Broom Tree], of the *Genji monogatari* [Tale of Genji], the famous eleventh-century prose romance by Lady Murasaki Shikibu (see catalog number 3), the story is told of a woman who bore a former lover a child. After a prolonged period apart, the woman sends the man a poem with a *nadeshiko* attached, in which the flower represents the child that she has borne:

*Yamagatsu no
kaki wa aru to mo
oriori ni
aware wa kakeyo
nadeshiko no tsuyu*

The border of the faux-woven cane is depicted.

Although the mountain
rustic's hedge may be tattered
every now and then
may the gentle dew come down
softly on the wild child-pink

The former lover returns the message, using a different word, *tokonatsu*, for the flower:

*Saki majiru
hana wa izure to
wakanedo mo
nao tokonatsu ni
shikumono zo naki*

The signature and seal of Shosai. The woven cane effect is noted as the background.

Although I can't choose
one flower from this luxuriant
nosegay of wild flowers
all the same to me there's no
bloom to match the carnation.

Shirayama Shōsai (1853-1923) was a leading lacquer master and educator of the Meiji (1868-1912) and Taisho (1912-26) periods. On this piece he has utilized a technique which gives the pipecase the appearance of woven cane. He emphasizes this effect by showing the border of the weaving in the upper portion of the pipecase. Using the name Fukumatsu, Shōsai exhibited a number of lacquer objects at the World's Columbian Exposition in Chicago in 1893 and from this time his reputation in Japan and in the West was established.

### Reference:

Brinkley, Frank, *Artistic Japan at Chicago: A Description of Japanese Works of Art Sent to the World's Fair* (Yokohama, 1893).

Gōke, Tadaomi, Hutt, Julia, and Wrangham, E. A., *Meiji no Takara, Treasures of Imperial Japan, Lacquer* (London, 1995), cat. no. 109, another pipe-case by Shōsai.

Japan Society and Suntory Museum of Art: *Autumn Grasses and Water: Motifs in Japanese Art from the Suntory Museum of Art* (exhibition catalog, New York, Japan House Gallery, fall 1983; New York, 1983), 26-8.

# BIBLIOGRAPHY

Abe Ikuji *et. al.*, *Shitsugei nyūmon* [An introduction to lacquer art] (Tokyo, 1972).

Abrams, H.N. (pub.), *Lacquer: An International History and Illustrated Survey* (New York, 1984).

Addiss, Stephen (ed.), *Japanese Ghosts and Demons: Art of the Supernatural* (exhibition catalog, June 13-September 1, 1985; New York and Lawrence, Kansas, 1985).

[Anon.], 'Hōmon-roku Shibata Reisai-shi [Account of a visit to Mr Shibata Reisai]', *Nihon shikkōkai zasshi* [Journal of the Japan Lacquer Association] (1907).

[Anon.], *Ausstellung Japan. Kunstwerke. Waffen. Schwertzieraten. Lacke. Gewebe. Holzschnitte. Sammlung Moslé* (Berlin, 1909).

Arakawa Hirokazu, *The Gō Collection of Netsuke* (Tokyo, 1983).

Araki Tadasu, *Dai Nihon shoga meika taikan* [A dictionary of Japanese painters and calligraphers] (Tokyo, 1934).

Bernard, Donald R., *The Life and Times of John Manjiro* (New York, 1992).

Boyer, Martha, *Catalogue of Japanese Lacquers* [in the Walters Art Gallery] (Baltimore, 1970).

Brinker, Helmut, *Zen in the Art of Painting* (London and New York, 1987).

Brinkley, Frank, *Artistic Japan at Chicago: A Description of Japanese Works of Art Sent to the World's Fair* (Yokohama, 1893).

Burlington Fine Arts Club, *Exhibition of Japanese Lacquer and Metal Work* (London, 1894).

Burmester, Andreas, 'Technical Studies of Japanese Lacquer', in Bromelle, N. S., and Smith, Perry (eds.), *Urushi* (Proceedings of the Urushi Study Group, June 10-27, 1985, Tokyo; Marina del Rey, Calif., 1988), 163-88.

Bushell, Raymond, *The Inrō Handbook* (New York and Tokyo, 1979).

Carpenter, Janet, 'The Immortals of Taoism', in Addiss, Stephen (ed.), *Japanese Ghosts and Demons: Art of the Supernatural* (exhibition catalog, June 13-September 1, 1985; New York and Lawrence, Kansas, 1985), 57-65.

Chamberlain, Basil H., *A Handbook for Travellers in Japan* (London, 1901).

Chamberlain, Basil H., *Things Japanese* (fourth edition; London, 1902).

Chan, Wing-Tsit, *A Source Book in Chinese Philosophy* (Princeton, 1963).

Clark, Timothy, *Demon of Painting: The Art of Kawanabe Kyōsai* (exhibition catalog, British Museum, December 1, 1993-February 13, 1994; London, 1993).

Davey, Neil K., and Tripp, Susan, *The Garrett Collection, Japanese Art: Lacquer, Inrō, Netsuke* (London, 1993).

Dilworth, David and Rimer, J. Thomas (eds.), 'Saiki Kōi', in *The Historical Fiction of Mori Ōgai* (Honolulu, 1977).

Dresser, Christopher, *Japan: Its Architecture, Art and Art Manufactures* (London, 1882).

Du, Yumin, 'The Production and Use of Chinese Raw Urushi and the Present State of Research', in Bromelle, N. S., and Smith, Perry (eds.), *Urushi* (Proceedings of the Urushi Study Group, June 10-27, 1985, Tokyo; Marina del Rey, Calif., 1988), 189-97.

Ducros, Alain, *Netsuke & Sagemono 1* (Granges-les-Valence, 1978)

Ducros, Alain, *Netsuke & Sagemono 2* (Granges-les-Valence, 1987).

Earle, Joe and Gōke, Tadaomi, *Meiji no Takara, Treasures of Imperial Japan, Masterpieces by Shibata Zeshin* (London, 1996).

Earle, Joe, 'Genji Meets Yang Guifei: A Group of Japanese Export Lacquers', *Transactions of the Oriental Ceramic Society*, 47 (1982-3), 45-75.

Earle, Joe (ed.), *The Toshiba Gallery: Japanese Art and Design* [in the Victoria and Albert Museum] (London, 1986).

Eskenazi Limited, *Japanese Netsuke from the Carré Collection* (exhibition catalog, June 15-July 9, 1993; London, 1993).

Fontein, Jan, and Hickman, Money L., *Zen Painting and Calligraphy* (exhibition catalog, November 5-December 20, 1970; Boston and Greenwich, Connecticut, 1970).

Foulds, Martin, 'Zeshin's Life and Works', in Link, Howard A., *The Art of Shibata Zeshin* (Honolulu, 1979), 19-30.

Garner, Harry, *Chinese Lacquer* (London, 1979).

Gilbertson, E., *et al.*, *A Japanese Collection Made by Michael Tomkinson* (London, 1898).

Glendining and Co., auction catalog of the W. L. Behrens Collection [by H. L. Joly], pt. ii. Lacquer and Inro (London, 1914).

Gōke, Tadaomi, Hutt, Julia, and Wrangham, E.A., *Meiji no Takara, Treasures of Imperial Japan, Lacquer* (London, 1995).

Gōke Tadaomi, 'Shitsugei no sui: Zeshin sakuhin [The essence of lacquer art: works by Zeshin]', *Me no me*, 241 (October 1996), 21-8.

Gōke Tadaomi, *Shibata Zeshin eyō tebikae* [Sketches and notes by Shibata Zeshin] (Tokyo, 1981).

Gonse, Louis, *L'art Japonais* (Paris, 1886).

Goodrich, L. Carrington, *Dictionary of Ming Biography* (New York and London, 1976).

Inaba Tsūryū Shin'emon, *Sōken Kishō* [Strange and wonderful sword-fittings], vol. 6 (partly reproduced in Arakawa Hirokazu, *The Gō Collection of Netsuke* (Tokyo, 1983); Osaka, 1781).

Jahss, Melvin and Betty, *Inrō, and Other Miniature Forms of Japanese Lacquer Art* (London, 1971).

Japan Society and Suntory Museum of Art: *Autumn Grasses and Water: Motifs in Japanese Art from the Suntory Museum of Art* (exhibition catalog, New York, Japan House Gallery, fall 1983; New York, 1983).

Jirka-Schmitz, Patrizia, 'Trompe-l'oeil, simulation and imitation in the decorative arts of the Meiji period', *Andon*, 7/27-8 (1987), 73-85.

Joly, Henri L. and Tomita, Kumasaku, *Japanese Art and Handicraft, Loan Exhibition Held in Aid of the British Red Cross* (London, 1916).

Joly, Henri L., *Legend in Japanese Art* (London, 1908).

Jordan, Brenda, 'The Trickster in Japan: *Tanuki* and *Kitsune*', in Addiss, Stephen (ed.), *Japanese Ghosts and Demons: Art of the Supernatural* (exhibition catalog, June 13-September 1, 1985; New York and Lawrence, Kansas, 1985), 129-37.

Jordan, Brenda, '*Yurei*: Tales of Female Ghosts', in Addiss, Stephen (ed.), *Japanese Ghosts and Demons: Art of the Supernatural* (exhibition catalog, June 13-September 1, 1985; New York and Lawrence, Kansas, 1985), 25-33.

Kobayashi, Tadashi, *Ukiyo-e* (Tokyo, New York, and San Francisco, 1982).

Kress, Heinz, 'Inro Motifs, Part I', *Netsuke Kenkyukai Journal*, 14/2 (Summer 1994), 24-37.

Kress, Heinz, 'Inro Motifs, Part III', *Netsuke Kenkyukai Journal*, 14/4 (Winter 1994), 20-42.

Kumanotani, J., 'The Chemistry of Oriental Lacquer', in Bromelle, N. S., and Smith, Perry (eds.), *Urushi* (Proceedings of the Urushi Study Group, June 10-27, 1985, Tokyo; Marina del Rey, Calif., 1988), 243-51.

Kurokawa Mayori, 'Hompō fūzoku setsu [On Japanese costume]', *Kokka*, 5 (1895), 180-3.

Kyoto National Museum, *Ritsuō saiku* [Inlaid lacquerwork by Ritsuō] (Kyoto, 1992).

Kyoto National Museum, *Nihon no ishō* [Designs of Japan] (Kyoto, 1978).

Kyoto National Museum, *Jūhasseiki no Nihon bijutsu: kattō suru biishiki* [Japanese art in the eighteenth century: conflicting aesthetics] (exhibition catalog, February 6-March 11, 1990; Kyoto, 1990).

Kyoto National Museum, *Makie, shikkoku to ōgon no Nihonbi* [The beauty of black and gold Japanese lacquer] (Kyoto, 1995).

Laufer, Berthold, *Jade: A Study in Chinese Archaeology and Religion* (New York, 1974; original edn. Chicago, 1912).

Lazarnick, George, *Netsuke and Inrō Artists and How to Read Their Signatures* (Honolulu, 1982).

Lewis, Edmund J., 'Japanese Lacquer Art: What's in a Name?', *Netsuke Kenkyukai Journal*, 11/4 (Winter 1991), 17-24.

Link, Howard A., *The Art of Shibata Zeshin* (Honolulu, 1979).

Link, Howard A., *Exquisite Visions: Rimpa Paintings from Japan* (exhibition catalog by Tōru Shimbo, Honolulu Academy of Arts, 1980; Honolulu, 1980).

Matsuda Gonroku, *Urushi no hanashi* [About lacquer] (Tokyo, 1964).

Matsumoto Seichō, *Tsuyoki ari* [The powerful ant] (Tokyo, 1974).

Mayer, Fanny H., *Ancient Tales in Modern Japan* (Bloomington, Indiana, 1984).

Meech, Julia, *Lacquerware from the Weston Collection, A Selection of Inro and Boxes* (New York, 1995).

Michener, James A., *The Floating World* (Honolulu, 1983; original edn. New York, 1954).

Miner, Earl, Odagiri, Hiroko, and Morrell, Robert E. *The Princeton Companion to Classical Japanese Literature* (Princeton, 1985).

Mizuo, Hiroshi, *Edo Painting: Sotatsu and Korin* (The Heibonsha Survey of Japanese Art, 18; New York and Tokyo, 1978).

Murasaki Shikibu, *The Tale of Genji* (trans. E. G. Seidensticker; London, 1976).

Murase, Miyeko, *Iconography of the Tale of Genji: Genji Monogatari Ekotoba* (New York and Tokyo, 1983).

Nicol, Clive W., *Harpoon: A Novel* (New York, 1987).

Oriental Ceramic Society, *Chinese Ivories from the Shang to the Qing* (exhibition catalog, British Museum, May 24-August 19, 1984; London, 1984).

Pekarik, Andrew J., *Japanese Lacquer, 1600-1900: Selections from the Charles A. Greenfield Collection* (exhibition catalog, New York, Metropolitan Museum of Art, September 4-October 19, 1980; New York, 1980).

Rein, Johannes Justus, *Japan nach Reisen und Studien im Auftrag der Königlich Preußischen Regierung*, ii. *Land und Forstwirtschaft, Industrie und Handel* (Leipzig, 1886) [English edn.: *The Industries of Japan* (New York and London, 1889)].

Rokkaku Shisui, *Tōyō shikkōshi* [A history of Far Eastern lacquerwork] (Tokyo, 1932).

Sawaguchi Goichi, *Nihon shikkō no kenkyū* [A study of Japanese lacquer] (Tokyo, 1933).

Schneeberger, Pierre-F., *Japanese Lacquer (Selected Pieces)* [in the Baur Collection, Geneva] (Geneva, 1984).

Shu Xincheng and others (ed.), *Cihai* [Chinese dictionary] (Shanghai, 1947).

Smithers, Peter, 'Moutan', *Arts of Asia*, 14/2 (March-April 1984), 55-61.

Takao Yō, 'Kinsei makie-shi meikan 4 [A list of Edo- and Meiji-period *maki-e* artists]', *Rokusho*, 17-20 (1996).

Takeuchi Kyūichi, 'Ritsuō seisaku no kōkeisha [The inheritors of the Ritsuō style]', *Shoga kottō zasshi* [Painting and antiques magazine] (Apr. 1916), 25-9.

Tanaka, Tomikichi, 'History of Tobacco Pouches', *Netsuke Kenkyukai Journal*, 10/4 (Winter 1990), 8-17.

Tanaka Ichimatsu *et. al.* (ed.), *Suiboku bijutsu taikei 4: Ryōkai, Intara* [A collection of ink-painting 4: Liang Kai and Intuoluo] (Tokyo, 1978).

Terajima Ryōan, *Wakan sansai zue* [Illustrated Japanese-Chinese encyclopedia of the three realms] (Tokyo, 1970; original edn. Osaka, 1716).

Tokugawa Art Museum, *Koboku* [Old carbon ink sticks in the Tokugawa Art Museum] (Kyoto, 1991).

Tokyo National Research Institute of Cultural Properties, *Naikoku kangyō hakurankai bijutsuhin shuppin mokuroku* [Catalogs of objects exhibited at the National Industrial Expositions] (Tokyo, 1996).

Tsang, Gerard, and Moss, Hugh, 'Scholar, Sage and Monk in Chinese Art: In Pursuit of the Absolute', in Oriental Ceramic Society of Hong Kong, *Arts from the Scholar's Studio* (exhibition catalog, Hong Kong, Fung Ping Shan Museum, October 24-December 13, 1986; Hong Kong, 1986).

Tokyo National Museum, *Tōkyō kokuritsu hakubutsukan zuhan mokuroku, shikkō chōdo-hen, bunbōgu* [Illustrated catalogs of Tokyo National Museum: lacquered furniture, stationery] (Tokyo, 1985).

Tsuda Noritake, untitled manuscript known as the 'Tsuda manuscript' (Tokyo, 1908) [privately produced English translation, 1986].

Tsuji, Nobuo, *Playfulness in Japanese Art* (The Franklin D. Murphy lectures, Spencer Museum of Art, University of Kansas, 1986; Lawrence, Kansas, 1986).

Tsunoda, Ryusaku *et. al.* (ed.), *Sources of Japanese Tradition* (New York and London, 1964).

Ueda, Reikichi, *The Netsuke Handbook of Ueda Reikichi* (adapted by Raymond Bushell; Rutland, Vt., and Tokyo, 1961).

Vergez, Robert, *Early Ukiyo-e Master: Okumura Masanobu* (Tokyo and New York, 1983).

Von Ragué, Beatrix, 'Materialien zu Iizuka Tōyō, seinem Werk und seiner Schule', *Oriens Extremus*, 11/2 (December 1964), 163-235.

Von Ragué, Beatrix, 'Inro Research: Some Proposed Future Steps', in Bromelle, N. S., and Smith, Perry (eds.), *Urushi* (Proceedings of the Urushi Study Group, June 10-27, 1985, Tokyo; Marina del Rey, Calif., 1988), 23-9.

Wakayama Hōmatsu (Takeshi), *Kinkō jiten* [A dictionary of sword-fitting makers] (Tokyo, 1972).

Waley, Arthur, *The Nō Plays of Japan* (London, 1921).

Watson, William (ed.), *The Great Japan Exhibition: Art of the Edo Period* (Exhibition catalogue, London, Royal Academy of Arts, October 24, 1981-February 21, 1982; London, 1981).

Williams, C. A. S., *Outlines of Chinese Symbolism and Art Motives* (Rutland, Vermont, 1974; original edn. Shanghai, 1941).

Winter, J., 'Pigments in China - a preliminary bibliography of identifications', in ICOM Committee for Conservation, Seventh Triennial Meeting, Copenhagen, II: 84.19.

Wrangham, E. A., *The Index of Inrō Artists* (Harehope, Northumberland, 1995).

Wu, Cheng-en, *Monkey*, trans. Arthur Waley (London, 1942).

Yonemura, Ann, *Japanese Lacquer* [in the Freer Gallery of Art] (Washington DC, 1979).